STAND BY FOR LOVE

Leslie and Jeff got up to clear their dishes from the table while Matt and Erin lingered over their Cokes.

"I wanted to ask you something," Matt said. "If you haven't already promised someone else, would you be my partner for the project?"

Erin breathed a sigh of relief. Evidently she had not totally disgraced herself that day.

"Partners?" Matt asked, standing up and holding out his hand.

"Partners," Erin agreed, feeling the warmth of his hand closing over hers.

"Are you two coming?" asked Leslie, a knowing smile on her face.

Erin blushed and quickly dropped Matt's hand. But Matt didn't seem to mind. As they walked out of the booth, his hand rested lightly on the back of her neck.

Now she'd have a chance to show him that she had a lot of good ideas. Most of all, Erin would have a chance to spend more time with Matt Blakeslee.

Bantam Sweet Dreams Romances
Ask your bookseller for the books you have missed

Stand By For Love

Carol Macbain

BANTAM BOOKS
TORONTO • NEW YORK • LONDON • SYDNEY • AUCKLAND

RL 6, IL age 11 and up

STAND BY FOR LOVE
A Bantam Book / December 1987

Cover photo by Pat Hill.

ISBN 0-553-26903-8

Published simultaneously in the United States and Canada

PRINTED IN THE UNITED STATES OF AMERICA

O   0 9 8 7 6 5 4 3 2 1

Stand By For Love

Chapter One

"Stand by—Quiet on the set, please!" The floor manager raised his arm as a signal for the crew and the guests seated under the bright lights to stop talking.

"Camera one, check your focus, quickly, please. Then zoom out a little." Erin Marksson listened to the instructions coming over her headset as she gripped the handles of the large studio camera mounted on a pedestal in front of her. She held it steady as she gazed into the viewfinder mounted on top.

"Camera one—" the voice began again.

Oops, That's me, she realized as she noticed the number one on the side of the cam-

1

era. Steadying the camera with her left hand, she groped for the manual zoom with her right. She rotated it in the wrong direction at first, then got her bearings, zoomed in on the guest's glasses, focused until she could read the tiny initials on the frames, then zoomed out again.

"Okay, camera one, hold that shot."

"Camera two. Pan a little to the left, please. The guest needs some more headroom."

Erin glanced at camera two. Her best friend, Leslie D'Amico was looking a little unsure of herself as she loosened the "pan" and "tilt" knobs. Strands of her wavy black hair were beginning to escape the red- and white-striped scarf that held back her thick ponytail. A serious expression had replaced her usual crinkly-eyed smile.

That afternoon was the first hands-on experience at the studio for Erin, Leslie, and Leslie's boyfriend, Jeff Reilly. They were part of a group of junior honor students from all over New England Cable's broadcast area who had been selected to serve as interns at the station during the fall semester. After two weeks of classroom instruction and a brief workshop to familiarize them with the studio cameras, the interns had begun to serve as crew-in-training for programs produced by organizations and residents of their large Boston suburb.

Erin could hear the calm voice of their instructor in the control room giving last-minute instructions to the crew. "Get ready to roll tape. Okay, roll it. Camera one, you're up first. Hold your shot. Ready. Bring up their mikes. Cue them."

The floor manager brought down his upraised arm, pointing to the first speaker as a signal for the show to begin.

"Hello, I'm Estelle Freeman. Today on 'Symposium' we're here to talk about the latest developments in joint replacement surgery with Dr. . . ."

The voice faded into the background as more directions from the control room demanded Erin's attention. "Get a close-up of those bones. Pull back for a two-shot. More headroom, camera one." The new terms were whirling around in her brain.

When she had signed up for this video course the past spring, Erin had hoped it would be easy. No long papers. No hours of research in the library. No memorizing long lists of strange words. She hadn't counted on video jargon. Not only that, if she messed up, she couldn't quietly take her F paper and throw it away. Here her mistakes would be made in public. The entire audience of cable subscribers would notice her jerky zooms and lapses in concentration.

At first the time went quickly. Camera one was supposed to cover the guest, Dr. Morse, and Erin had to move around frequently to get close-ups of the X rays and artificial hips the doctor had brought. It kept her busy. After a while she realized her whole body was aching. The camera was heavy, and her muscles were tense from trying to hold it perfectly still—sometimes with one hand, if she needed to focus or zoom. It occurred to Erin that she should have spent more time in the swimming pool last summer building up muscles and less time in front of the TV set to have properly prepared for this course!

Halfway through the show a tape was shown of Dr. Morse replacing a finger joint. Taking advantage of this short break, Erin locked her camera into position so she could let go of it for a moment. She wiggled her slender shoulders around and then fell forward, rounding her back until her dark blond hair almost touched the floor. She stayed bent over for a minute, letting her shoulder and back muscles go limp to get rid of the stiffness. As she stood up, she glanced over at the monitor just as the surgeon's knife peeled the flesh away from someone's joint. *Yuck, I'm not ready for this,* she thought, looking quickly away.

When she turned around, she could see into the control room at the back of the studio. Poised in front of a whole wall of TV screens was that day's assistant director, a tall, handsome boy who wore his headset over a mop of long, black curls. He stood next to Eve Stratford, their instructor, and pushed the buttons on the control panel in response to her commands. He didn't look nervous at all, Erin observed.

She listened to his funny comments through her earphones, desperately trying not to laugh as the staff in the control room joked around. The camera crew wasn't allowed to make the slightest sound after shooting began—they couldn't even sneeze or clear their throat because the sound would be picked up by the sensitive microphones.

"Unlock your cameras now. We're ready to continue," came the warning.

As Dr. Morse droned on and on, Erin's mind drifted from the job at hand. She tried to follow the director's instructions exactly, wanting to do her best, but she found herself listening for the assistant's voice above the others, trying to catch a quick glimpse of him over her shoulder when she wasn't busy.

"Give them the three-minute cue." The floor manager waved three fingers in the air until the host acknowledged the signal with a slight nod.

At last it was almost over.

The muscles around Erin's shoulder blades were in knots again. Erin was short and small boned, and the strain of balancing the heavy camera at such an uncomfortable angle had taken its toll. In addition to that discomfort, she was getting a chill. Her hands were sweaty from anxiety, but her body was shaking from the cold. It had to be well under sixty degrees in the studio.

It had been warm and sunny when she left home that afternoon, and she had worn her pretty hand-painted T-shirt and a light jacket, which she tossed in the corner of the studio after she had arrived. Now, as she looked around, she saw that the old hands were wearing long-sleeved wool sweaters. It seemed there were quite a few survival tips that had been omitted from the textbook.

"Okay. That's it. Good job, everybody. Lock your cameras and put the lens caps back on," came the final instructions from the control room as the bright studio lights faded down and the regular lights flipped on.

As the colored background lighting and the unlit shadows gave way to ordinary light, the illusion of a comfortable office created by the set disappeared. The chairs and table on the deserted platform now looked out of place against the stark white walls of the studio. The oversize room, almost as large as a small gym, was cluttered with chairs and tables, and with all the various platforms, boxes, curtains, and equipment used to create sets for other shows pushed to one side. Erin replaced her lens cap and slowly rolled camera one over to its place beside the control room door.

"The show went pretty well today, didn't it?"

Erin turned quickly as she heard the familiar voice, and found herself looking up into a pair of intense dark eyes.

"I didn't get a chance to introduce myself before the show. I'm Matt Blakeslee. You must be 'camera one.' "

"Um-hmm, also known as Erin Marksson,"

she said with a grin, stuffing her hands nervously into the pockets of her white jeans as she felt his gaze on her face.

"You guys did a pretty good job for your first time behind the camera," Matt said. "Eve only lost her temper twice," he added, grinning.

"Really? You're serious?"

"Well, maybe three times," he said, joking. "No, really, your shots were all pretty smooth. And you followed directions quickly, which is important. Yesterday the crew kept trying to get fancy and do their own thing. Eve hates that. She stopped the show and gave everyone a lecture."

"You worked on yesterday's show, too?" Erin asked, pushing a lock of straight blond hair back behind her ear.

"Yeah, this is my second time pushing the buttons. I love it. It's really fun."

"You looked as if you'd been doing it for ages," Erin said. "How can you be so relaxed?"

"Well, I *was* pretty tense at first," he said, leaning back against the wall and crossing his arms over his chest. He gave her a cocky grin. "But I tried not to let it show."

"The way I did," Erin said with a moan. "About the only thing that helped keep me calm was your joking."

"I always crack jokes when I'm nervous," Matt said kindly. "Eve doesn't mind. She says that's better than getting angry, because if the director gets flustered, everybody else gets nervous and the show really starts to fall apart."

"I think I'd better start helping the others put some of this stuff away." Erin was reluctant to end the conversation, but she was running out of things to say.

"I'd better pitch in, too. Eve gets sort of crazy if everything isn't put back exactly right."

"Thanks for the tip."

"Sure. Hope I'll see you again soon."

"Me, too," Erin added shyly.

While she helped lug the huge potted plants that had lined the set back into the hall, Erin watched Matt out of the corner of her eye. He neatly coiled up the twisted blue microphone cables and stacked them in the cabinet. Then he climbed the mobile platform and began removing the gels from the lights that had flooded the back wall with color. He pulled himself and the platform along by the bars of the light grid along the high ceiling and expertly removed the thin blue and green filters from in front of the bulbs. Erin was really impressed. Matt seemed to know exactly how to do everything.

What was even more impressive was that he seemed to leave everyone he talked to in a good mood. Erin found she couldn't take her eyes off him. Their eyes met once, but she looked away quickly, not wanting to be caught staring. She was definitely attracted to this Matt Blakeslee. Erin replayed their conversation in her mind and hoped he wasn't just being polite when he had said he hoped to see her again.

Finally the studio was back to normal, a huge, empty, white-walled space. All signs of the recent frenzy of activity were now totally erased.

Erin retrieved her jacket and school bag and went out to find Jeff and Leslie in the crowd around the soda machine in the hall.

"That's it," Jeff exclaimed when he spotted Erin. He downed the last drop of his soda and tossed the empty can away. "Let's hit the road. I still have a science exam to study for this evening."

As they opened the door onto the street, Erin felt the warm rays of the late-afternoon sun. "Would you believe it's practically hot out? My hands and feet are freezing from all that air-conditioning," she said, complaining.

"The equipment comes first around there. They say video cameras thrive in a nice chilly room," Jeff explained as he pulled his gray sweatshirt off.

"Well, I sure don't. Please don't ever let me leave home again without at least two sweaters," Erin said. "And my back is killing me, too."

"Those cameras *do* get heavy after a while," Jeff agreed, flexing his muscles. "Even a strong dude like me can feel it."

"Do you think we're tough enough for this course?" Leslie asked, laughing as she looked down at her thin arms and long slender fingers. "Maybe there should have been a physical."

"Well, it's too late now. We're stuck for the rest of the semester, so we'd better shape up," Jeff said. "Or at least you two had better. I'm in pretty good shape myself."

He jumped up and grabbed for the lowest limb of one of the young maple trees that lined the sidewalk, easily chinning himself, then dropped lightly to the ground to rejoin the girls.

"I could do more," he said, grinning and

pushing his wavy brown hair back from his forehead, "but it's been a hard day."

"Show-off!" Leslie said as she put her hand on his muscular shoulder. "I guess we'll just have to rely on our superior brain power."

"I don't know about that," Erin said as they continued down the sidewalk. "I could hardly concentrate on the directions. It's hard to pay attention to the show and the control room at the same time."

"I can't keep all those new words straight, either," Leslie admitted. "Let's see, 'pan' means turn the camera and 'truck' means move the whole camera to one side or the other."

"Uh-oh," Jeff groaned. "I think I trucked when I was supposed to pan."

"You should have seen me zooming," Erin said, "I got so flustered I forgot to tilt up and almost cut off the guest's head. Good thing I got it centered up again before Matt switched to my shot. I think I'll get the hang of it, though, with a little more practice. Matt said I was good—and on my first day, too."

Leslie looked up as she noted a change in Erin's voice. "Ah-ha! I think I detect a spark of interest here. How about it, Erin?"

Erin blushed slightly. One of the disadvantages of having such a fair complexion, in addition to having to wear gobs of sunscreen whenever she went to the beach, was that she blushed very easily. Her clear pale skin gave away her emotions instantly.

"I thought so!" Leslie teased. "The love bug has bitten again."

"Come on, Les, I just met him," Erin protested. "I'm not in love."

"Maybe not yet—but he *is* cute, that's for sure."

"Wait a minute! Wait a minute!" Jeff joined in, laughing. "Leslie, you're not supposed to be going around thinking about who is cute. There's only one 'cute' guy you have to worry about, and he's right here."

Leslie rolled her eyes and gave him a quick hug. "Isn't he awful?" she said, turning to Erin. "He's so conceited. Just because he has these beautiful, big brown eyes he thinks I shouldn't even notice anyone else."

"Well, you can notice. Just don't get me nervous about it," Jeff replied.

"Don't worry, I'm not the one interested in Matt. It's Erin, remember? I was just remarking on her good taste, that's all."

This was enough to make Erin blush again. "Come on, you're embarrassing me."

"Okay, okay. Not another word about you-know-who," Leslie promised. "Let's get on home."

Jeff and Leslie joined hands and walked on ahead, talking about their plans for the weekend while Erin lagged behind with thoughts and images from the afternoon going through her head. Her hopes for the future were high. Her first experience at the studio was everything she had hoped it would be—and more.

Chapter Two

Erin opened the door to the front hall and was immediately confronted by her younger brother, Davy, who was precariously balanced in the doorway to the kitchen. One bare foot was pressed flat against either side of the door jamb about four feet from the floor, leaving him suspended in the open doorway, his tousled blond curls about a foot from the top. He folded his arms and grinned triumphantly. Only the pressure of his legs pushing against the sides of the door jamb kept him from crashing down to the floor.

"Bet you didn't know I could climb the walls, did you?" he asked.

"No, but it's a pretty good stunt," Erin said agreeably, as she ducked down under him to get to the kitchen.

"I want to be on TV. Can I do this on your show? Can I?" he pleaded.

"Well, I don't think it's quite—" she began.

"A lot of kids would probably like to see me do this," he said, interrupting.

Ever since Erin had started talking about the video course, seven-year-old Davy had been badgering her with schemes to get on TV. He wanted to sing; he wanted to tell jokes; he wanted to do stunts. Anything to get into the limelight.

He always looked so disappointed when she had to reject his ideas. In a way, though, she could understand how he felt. Anything having to do with TV *was* exciting, even if it was just a small local station.

"Davy, get down from there," called their mother from the kitchen. "You'll mark up the walls!"

Davy made a face but did as he was told. He jumped down and raced over to the cookie jar for a snack, while Erin sat down at the kitchen table where Mrs. Marksson was slicing tomatoes from their garden into a large wooden salad bowl.

"Tell me about your taping session this afternoon," her mother said.

"It was great. Scary at first, but fun." Her body was miserable, still stiff and aching, but Erin happily related her day's events. "It was just an interview with a doctor, but I got to cover the guest, which was neat because I had to get close-ups of the bones and artificial knees and stuff that he brought. I did a lot of zooming, too, which is the hardest thing."

"How do you figure out what to do?" her mother asked.

"Oh, that's easy. We wear headsets so the director in the control room can give us directions. He tells us if he wants a close-up or a long shot or if we need to focus or anything. Then he switches back and forth among the cameras to whoever has the most interesting spot. He used mine a lot," she added.

"I'd love to see it, Erin. When will it be on?"

"I'm not sure, but I think it'll be Thursday night. I'll check the Guide."

"We'll make sure to watch it," Mrs. Marksson promised as she poured the dressing over the salad.

"It's hard, but it's fun. I can't wait till the next session," Erin said, excitement sparkling in her pale blue eyes. "Our teacher, Eve, goes way back to the old TV days. She's worked for all the different networks and told us some really funny stories about her first job on the old Jackie Gleason show. That was when everything was live, and she had to get all the props ready."

"That does sound interesting," her mother agreed. "A teacher with a lot of experience makes the best instructor."

"Yeah, she really knows what she's doing. She's tough, but she's funny, too. It won't seem like work even if we do have to go three times a week, plus the extra sessions when we start our own projects."

Erin reached to take the dishes out of the cupboard and began to set the table as she chatted.

"Leslie and Jeff like it as much as I do. Leslie even said she was glad I talked her into it, although now she'll have to practice her piano before school instead of after."

"Who else is in the class?" her mother asked.

"Oh, about ten other kids from Ashboro High, and the rest are from private schools, I guess."

"Maybe you'll make some new friends." Erin

smiled at her mother's suggestion. That was just what she had in mind!

Erin's second session at the studio later in the week was more relaxed. She had gotten the feel of the camera and could follow the director's instructions almost without thinking. Matt was assisting in the control room, getting the tapes cued up so they would be at the right place when they were needed and setting up the credits that would be flashed on the screen at the end of the show.

In between takes, Erin would glance over at the control room, trying to get a glimpse of Matt. Once he caught her eye and gave her a quick smile and a wave—it made her day.

From then on Erin went to the studio every chance she got, even signing up for extra sessions when the crews were short of help.

One afternoon she came in to observe the audio board, hoping to learn something about how to balance the level of voices with the music so that everything sounded good together. Luckily, or perhaps unluckily, Matt was directing again.

Erin sat next to the audio technician, trying her hardest to pay attention to the knobs he was turning, but her eyes kept wandering back to Matt. And Matt seemed to know it. Twice she caught him looking at her, laughing, as if to say, "What are you doing over there, anyway?"

Finally the program ended. Erin's heart began to pound when she saw Matt give her a warm smile and start walking toward her. She could barely hide her disappointment when Eve intercepted him, calling him aside.

Later that evening while Erin was trying to catch up on her other schoolwork, the phone rang. She started to get it but was nearly run over by Davy who raced ahead of her.

"Why did the mad scientist bury the battery?" Davy began as soon as he picked up the phone. He smiled smugly, shaking his head as he listened. "Nope! Because it was dead. What did the mad scientist get when he crossed a frog with a soft drink?"

After a slight pause he answered, "Wrong again! It's Croak-a-Cola!"

"Davy, who are you talking to?" Erin asked.

"I don't know. Someone for you."

"You mean that call is for me and you're standing there telling mad-scientist jokes?" Erin leapt off the couch and grabbed for the phone.

"I think he liked them," Davy said indignantly.

"Hello?"

"Hi. May I speak to Erin, please?"

"This is Erin."

"Oh, hi. This is Matt Blakeslee. Glad I finally got hold of you. Thought I'd dialed another wrong number. I tried two other Marksssons before I found you. That double *s* had me fooled for a while."

"You have the right number this time, but I'm afraid you just had a conversation with my little brother."

"At least he knows some good jokes," Matt said with a laugh.

"Maybe if you're hearing them for the first time," Erin admitted. "They're getting a little old around here."

"I bet you learned a lot about audio this afternoon," Matt said teasingly. "That was a good idea to just come and watch, but you seemed a little distracted."

"Guess I was just a little spaced out," Erin said, feeling herself blush. She hoped Matt wouldn't guess what it was that had distracted her.

"Anyway," Matt said a little tentatively. "I wondered if you'd like to come over after school sometime. I have a pretty big video collection, and we could watch a few old favorites."

Erin couldn't believe her ears. It was really Matt Blakeslee asking her over. Her heart was racing, but she tried to sound cool and casual.

"Sure. That would be great. When do you want to get together?"

"I'm free tomorrow. How about you?"

Erin hoped she didn't sound too eager. "Hmm, let's see. I guess tomorrow would be okay. Where do you live?"

"Over on West Hill Drive, near the top of the hill."

Matt's neighborhood was a good five miles from hers. She didn't really want to ask her mother to drive her over there.

"Gee, Matt, I don't know—"

"Don't worry, I'll pick you up on my way home from school. Then you won't have any trouble finding it. You're not far out of my way."

"What school do you go to?" Erin asked. "I don't think I've ever seen you around Ashboro High."

"I go to the Preston Academy for the Arts, so I usually drive every day."

Erin was impressed. Preston Academy was

a very expensive and exclusive school for kids with special artistic talent. There was always something in the paper about a Preston student winning an award or being chosen to perform somewhere special.

"I'm usually home from school by three o'clock. Stop by anytime after that, and I'll be ready to go," Erin said.

"Okay, then, it's a date. See you tomorrow around three. Hey"—Matt sounded as if he didn't want the conversation to end—"will I get to see this brother of yours?"

"Unfortunately, yes. But I'll try to keep it as brief as possible. If he finds out you're also in the video course, he'll probably try to get you to watch one of his acts. He thinks the public is dying to see him perform."

"What? He wants to see my act?" Davy asked. "Tell him I'm ready anytime."

"Uh-oh, he heard me. I'm afraid you're in for it now."

She heard Matt laugh. "That's okay. I'll tell him sick chicken jokes."

"Just what he needs," Erin murmured with a smile. She'd even put up with chicken jokes if they came from Matt.

"Well, I'll see you tomorrow," Matt said. "Okay?"

"Okay. 'Bye."

She put the phone down and nearly hugged herself. This was more than she had hoped for—an invitation to Matt's house. The very next day. She went back to her place on the couch and relaxed into the oversize pillows, closing her eyes. As she absentmindedly twisted her long hair around her fingers, she pictured Matt—his thick, dark curls and laughing eyes. She remembered the way he shrugged his strong shoulders and stuffed his hands into the big square pockets of his baggy gray pants. What a hunk!

The door between the garage and the kitchen slammed shut. Erin looked up as her father came into the living room.

"Hi, there," he said. "How are things in TV land?"

"Great, Dad," she said, hopping up from the couch to give him a quick hug. "I started learning audio today."

"You're really jumping right in, aren't you?" he said as he took off his jacket and loosened his tie.

Erin nodded. "I'm trying. I think I like doing camera best. It's more exciting. When you do audio you just keep your eyes glued to these little needles and make sure the sound doesn't

24

get too loud. It's important, but a little boring. What I like is 'lights, camera, *action.*' "

"I'd love to see you in action," her father said as he tossed his jacket over the back of the couch.

"Come over and see the studio sometime. Anyone can visit. It's really neat—state of the art. I'll show you around if you want," Erin offered cheerfully.

"Incredible. I never thought a child of mine would get into all this high-tech stuff," Mr. Marksson said. "I've always been a 'wood-stove' type myself. Next thing you know, you'll be wanting a computer."

"No, Dad, I don't need a computer, but—we could really use a VCR. I'm going to be getting assignments to watch certain shows, and if I could tape them and watch them later, no one would have to miss their favorites on my account. Wouldn't that be a good idea?"

"Well, I'll think it over," he promised. "But don't get your hopes up. There are a few things ahead of a VCR on my 'must buy' list."

"I'm really going to need one, Dad," she said, pressing. "After I finish my first project, I want to make a copy and send it to Gram and Grandpa."

Her father looked at her in surprise. "You're

taking all this pretty seriously, aren't you? I didn't realize you were so interested in TV."

"Well, I wasn't—because I didn't know about it before. I could never decide what I wanted to do because it didn't seem like I was really good at anything. I mean, I'm pretty good at most things but not outstanding at any one thing."

"I think it's a little early in the internship to know whether or not you're good," he said cautiously.

"I guess—but I've got a good feeling about this, Dad."

"Well, good for you. My daughter, the TV producer. I like the sound of it already." He put a hand on her shoulder. "Come on, let's get dinner started."

That night Erin lay in bed thinking over the day's events. It was hard to believe, but her life was actually starting to hang together very nicely.

At the beginning of their junior year, her friends at Ashboro High had begun thinking about college plans, and Erin had felt left out. Everyone else seemed to know where they were going, but she had no idea what she wanted to do with her life. Leslie was devoted

n sooner or later." Leslie said as she took
er place between them, linking her arm
ith theirs.

Erin told Jeff about her phone conversa
on with Matt as they strolled along the tree
ned street.

"Do you have time for a Coke?" Jeff aske
s they approached his family's rambling whit
ouse.

"Thanks, guys, but I have to get home an
y to get rid of Davy before Matt arrives. Ta
you later."

Erin continued down the street at a quick
ace as her friends headed around to th
eillys' side door.

As she passed the huge lilac bushes th
vided her yard from the one next door, h
ce fell. Davy and his best friend, Ben, we
the middle of a water-gun fight on th
nt lawn. Dressed in GI·Joe fatigues an
rying large automatic, pulsing water p
s, they were gleefully darting from bush
h in true commando fashion.

Davy, you've got to stop! Don't you do
my hair wet!"

on't worry, Erin," Davy answered. "We
trying to protect our base."

avy," Erin said sternly, "there's only o

to the piano and was interested in music
school; Jeff was sending away for information on colleges with computer programming
and good hockey teams; but Erin was adrift.
She had no all-consuming interest. She did
well in all her subjects and liked just about
everything, except softball. But she had never
devoted a lot of energy to any one thing. She
didn't have to. Things came easily for her.
Erin was used to being successful without
really trying.

This video course was going to be something she could really put her heart into. *In
more ways than one*, she thought, smiling
to herself as she drifted off to sleep.

Chapter Three

Erin went around in a daze all day Friday. She couldn't stop thinking about Matt coming to pick her up after school.

She hoped Davy would be out playing when he arrived. He was a little hard to explain to new friends—a little too whacky, even for a younger brother. Her mom said he was "creative," and her dad called him "energetic," but Erin thought what they really meant was "totally nutty." It'd be nice to get to know Matt a little better before exposing him to her brother's weird imitations. Unfortunately, Davy was convinced that everyone who came

to see her was dying to see his versi
frog dancing with a chicken.

"Erin! Erin, wait up!"

Leslie and Jeff were running to ca
with her. Jeff was jogging easily in spit
carrying both his books and Leslie's, a
lie was almost out of breath from the e
dashing across the school yard. Jeff
few doors away from Erin, and he an
usually went there to study after scho
three of them frequently walked ho
gether, but that day Erin had left in
to make sure she arrived home well a
Matt.

"Hey, what's the rush?" Jeff called

"Oh, I've got to get home early for an
school date," Erin said, smiling mischi

"You do! Why didn't you tell us? Wh
Where? Give us the details," he dem

"Never mind, Jeff," Leslie said, sco
"Erin's got to have some privacy."

"I bet I know," Jeff guessed. "It's
what's his name?"

"Blakeslee. Matt Blakeslee. He
come over to his house to watch s
Erin admitted.

"See, I kept your secret, bu
any good. Jeff always finds ou

thing I'm worried about, and it's *not* a commando raid. I've got a friend coming to pick
me up in a few minutes, and I want you two
to disappear. I mean vanish. Understand?"

"Understood, sir!" said Davy, giving a mock-
military salute before slipping back behind
the bushes.

Not much time left now, Erin thought as
she rushed inside and up to her room. She
dropped her books on her desk and ran a
comb through her long, silky hair.

Then she went down to the kitchen, ate
the two cookies remaining in the cookie jar,
and went into the living room to sit by the
front window to watch for Matt. She strained
to see each car as it approached. Her heart
raced as a red Porsche turned onto her street.
She was getting ready to reach for the door,
but it sped past. An old jalopy needing a new
muffler and a lot of body work approached
next. She was relieved when it kept on going.
A few more cars went by. Finally, a blue Saab
made its way slowly up the street, coming to
a stop across from her house.

It was Matt. As he got out of the car and
looked around to make sure of the house
number, she noticed Davy still hiding in the

bushes at the side of the yard. He was carefully taking aim.

Erin leaned out the window and called to Matt, "If I were you, I'd duck!"

"What?" he called back, coming toward the house.

She dashed to the front door. "Just don't come any closer," Erin warned as she closed the door behind her and headed for the car.

But it was too late. As she came down the walk, Davy shot two streams of water, the first just missing Matt, the second hitting her squarely in the back.

"Davy!" She whirled on her brother.

Davy, of course, was running off giggling with his friend. How could he do this to her on her first date with Matt?

Erin decided her best bet was to ignore the whole thing. She continued on across the street toward Matt, who was leaning against his car, an extremely amused expression on his face.

"That was some greeting," he said. "Looks like you're pretty well protected in this neighborhood. I think anyone would have trouble getting through with those two on guard duty," he added loudly enough for the boys to overhear.

Erin rolled her eyes. "*Please*, don't encourage them," she begged. "I knew Davy would pick today to do something crazy."

"Oh, they're just having fun. I used to do stuff like that, too, when I was a kid. I had an entire camouflage outfit and a walkie-talkie. Used to drive my sister, Jean, crazy. It was a lot of fun, actually."

He laughed as he ducked behind the car and pretended to return the boys' fire.

"I hope the mail carrier thinks it's as funny as you do, or we might have a problem," Erin replied as she climbed into the front seat.

"Oh, he won't mind. The boys don't bite, do they?"

"Not yet."

"I'm glad I was somebody else's younger brother," he confessed. "I never had to put up with one myself."

"Believe me, it's not easy."

He turned to her as he started the car. "Did he get you soaked?"

Erin smiled. "Not really. Just irritated."

Matt reached over and brushed a strand of hair from the side of her face. "Don't be. I kind of liked it. Made me feel very brave, rescuing you from the commandos."

They drove on in silence for a while, through

33

the downtown section, past some large apartment buildings, into an area of ample yards and winding roads. Matt pulled into a long, curving driveway that led around to the back of a stately red brick house.

"Here we are. Hop out."

As he opened the car door, an Irish setter bounded up and put one paw on his knee.

"Tim, boy. How you doing?" Matt said as he picked up a stick from the nearby wood-pile and tossed it high into the air. The dog paused, watching the stick fall in a tangle of small trees and bushes at the far end of the lot, then bounded off to retrieve it.

"What a view!" Erin said. "I didn't know you could see so much of the city from here." The backyard dropped off sharply, opening up a beautiful view of the Boston skyline. "It must be nice at night."

"Yeah. That's why we bought this house. My mom can't resist a beautiful view. Never mind that the roof leaked and the plumbing didn't work—if only she could see the sunrise. On the Fourth of July we can even see the fireworks over the river."

"Hmm, neat," Erin said a little enviously.

She sat on the edge of the patio next to a pot of red geraniums. Tim scrambled up the stone path edging the wildflower bed and dropped the stick at Erin's feet. As she bent over to accept his gift she felt the dog's rough, wet tongue on her cheek.

"You must like dogs," Matt said. "Tim can always spot a dog lover. But you don't have to keep throwing that stick for him. He'll keep you busy all afternoon. Come on in. It's video time."

Quietly followed by the well-trained setter, they climbed the stairs to the deck and crossed into a sunny room, where Mrs. Blakeslee was busy at her computer terminal.

"Hi, Mom. This is my friend, Erin, from the cable studio. She's one of the interns from Ashboro High."

"I'm so happy to meet you, Erin," Mrs. Blakeslee said, turning to greet them. "Matt has told me what a talented group of kids he's working with this fall."

Erin blushed slightly at the compliment.

"It's such a wonderful opportunity for you all. Matt was thrilled when he got the chance to work at the studio this term. I don't know if he's told you, but he did some outstanding video work last year at Preston Academy."

Now it was Matt's turn to look uncomfortable. "Oh, Mom . . ."

"I hope you'll excuse me, though," Mrs. Blakeslee went on as she glanced at the pile of notes next to the keyboard. "I've got a deadline tomorrow, and I really can't stop until this newsletter is done."

"That's okay, Mom." Matt sounded relieved as he led Erin out of the study. "We'll help ourselves to a snack."

They wandered into the kitchen, opened some sodas and a bag of chips, then began to browse through Matt's collection of tapes for something to watch.

"What do you like? Humor? Adventure? Bogart? Here's a list of everything we've got. My mom insisted on putting it all on the computer."

He handed her a list of titles filling several pages of perforated computer paper. The last item on the list was labeled *"Matt's Video— 'Skateboard City.' "*

"Hey, this looks interesting," Erin said, pointing to that entry. "Can I see it?"

Matt winced. "Don't believe my mother, Erin. It's no masterpiece."

"That's okay. I'd really like to see it."

"I spent hundreds of hours on it, but some things you just can't fix. I could probably do better now."

"Don't apologize. Just show it," Erin said. "I'll bet it's good."

He looked at her for a long moment, as if trying to decide whether he could trust her. "Okay," he said at last. "But tell me what you really think of it. Be honest. I can take it." He smiled. "Just don't be *too* brutal. Everyone has his limits."

"Don't worry, I'm very tactful," Erin assured him with a laugh. "Davy taught me how to be subtle."

He grinned back at her. "That's what I figured. Okay. Roll 'em." He popped the tape into the VCR.

A kid on a skateboard careened onto the screen. Racing toward the viewer, he turned abruptly and stopped, the bottom of the board lifted up to reveal a fire-breathing dragon. Then came another and another and another. The action was fast, bursting with energy, and the camera cut back and forth between the skateboarders, as they appeared to move to the background music. The opening sequence was followed by the kids talking and demonstrating different tricks, and then the action went to a tournament on a special course, a collage of helmets and knee pads, judges, triumphs, and, of course, spills.

It was short—less than fifteen minutes—but almost professional looking. Erin was awed.

"You really did the camera work and everything?" she asked.

"A friend from school helped me, but I did most of it myself—Do you like it?"

"Like it? I think it's terrific. You've got some great shots. That kid on the cobra board—wasn't he something?"

"He was super. He could do anything. And he was nice, too. He did a couple of things over a few times when I messed up on my camera shots. I really appreciated that."

"And that redheaded guy," Erin said, continuing. "It looked like he turned his board completely around while he was up in the air. I've never seen anyone do that before."

"You should have seen all the stuff he did! I didn't even get all of it. It came out kind of blurry."

When Matt started talking about his video, his face seemed to light up. Erin couldn't help getting excited about it along with him.

"I'm glad you liked it," he said as he rewound the tape. "My parents think *everything* I do is wonderful. On the other hand, some of the kids at school are so competitive they pick apart every little thing that isn't perfect just so *their* stuff will look better. So it's kind of hard to tell where you really stand. It means a lot to be able to show my work to someone who really appreciates it."

"I just hope someday I can do something *half* that good," Erin admitted.

She began looking through the list of tapes again.

"Would you like a summer love story?" Matt asked.

"Yeah, I'd like that," she said.

"Me, too," he said and started the tape. They leaned back into the pillows on the floor as the movie began. Casually, Matt put his arm around Erin's shoulders. And for the next hour and a half Erin was in heaven, a handsome boy by her side and a friendly dog at her feet.

Chapter Four

"I've been looking forward to this workshop all weekend," Erin confided to Leslie and Jeff as they walked the few blocks from the high school to the cable studio. The week before, Eve had announced that the students were ready to learn how to use the portable equipment they would need for their individual projects. "You know, this is the first time in my life I've looked forward to going back to school on Monday more than getting out on Friday."

"It is fun," Jeff agreed. "But not enough to make me look forward to Monday morning.

You know what, Les," he said, turning conspiratorially toward Leslie, "I think it's more than the thought of getting her hands on this high-tech equipment that's turning Erin on, don't you?"

"Hey, you promised not to tease," Erin said, pleading with him.

"That's right, Jeff," Leslie said. "If Erin gets up in the morning with a burning desire to hold a video camera, who are we to question it?" she asked, laughing and trying to duck behind Jeff as Erin reached out to give her dark, wavy ponytail a friendly tug.

"Come on, you two are ganging up on me. It's not fair. I really *am* excited about this workshop, and I can't wait to get started on my own project."

"It'll be neat going around town with all our video equipment. Do you think people will take us seriously?" Leslie wondered.

"I think we should get New England Cable sweatshirts and IDs," Erin said.

"I bet you've got your parnter all picked out already," Jeff said, needling Erin a little more.

"Well, I can dream, can't I?" Erin answered, smiling.

Leslie put an arm around Erin's shoulder.

"There's no harm in getting a little help from an expert," she said.

"You bet. Especially a tall, dark, good-looking expert," Jeff said sarcastically.

"Well, if you're real, real nice, I just might pass on a few pointers," Erin replied.

They arrived at the cable station along with several of the other members of their class. Together, they filed up the stairs to the studio area on the second floor. Everyone stashed their schoolbags under the chairs along the wall but then hung back nervously in small groups waiting for the class to begin.

Erin stuck close to Jeff and Leslie while scanning the other groups to see if Matt had arrived yet. There was no sign of him. But a few moments later he emerged from the storage room carrying an assortment of oddly shaped cases and large canvas bags. A bright orange, heavy-duty extension cord slid off of one shoulder as Matt set his burdens down. He looked around, smiling as he caught her eye, and Erin went over to say hello.

"Can I help out?" she asked.

"Sure, come on back here and grab a couple of these boxes of lights," Matt said, showing her the way.

She picked up a long, narrow black case

that felt more as if it were filled with bricks than lights. She half carried, half dragged it across the floor into the studio. Dutifully she went back for a second set of lights and felt extremely relieved when the workshop began and saved her from a third trip.

First came the rules and regulations—about ten pages of dos and don'ts and procedures. Then there were insurance forms and releases for their parents to sign. Then another packet was passed out with photocopied pictures and diagrams of the types of portable equipment they would be using. Unfortunately, these seemed to be copies of copies of copies and were barely legible.

I think I really will need an expert to figure this all out, Erin thought to herself, glancing at Matt who stood beside her.

"There sure is a lot of red tape," he whispered. "I wish they'd hurry up with it. I want to get my hands on this equipment."

But they spent the next hour listening carefully and watching demonstrations of how the various cameras, tripods, VCR decks, adapters, and monitors were set up. Erin tried to make notes on the materials that had been handed out, but the pictures and diagrams never seemed to correspond exactly with the actual equipment in front of her.

"It's complicated at first, but you'll pick it up after you try it a few times," Matt said reassuringly.

"Are you sure?" Erin replied, her enthusiasm slightly dampened by the reality of video technology.

"Sure, I'm sure. The first time is always confusing."

"Okay, everybody," Eve announced. "The demonstration is over. Grab a partner, find some equipment, and take turns setting it up. Call me when you've got everything working, and I'll check you out. Then break everything down and put it all back in the cases."

Erin's stomach felt a little queasy.

"Okay. Go to it," their instructor urged cheerily.

"Come on, Erin. Let's try this one," Matt decided as he picked up one of the bulky cameras. "I'll go first, okay? Then you try it."

Erin watched carefully as Matt began to plug in each piece of equipment. The main idea was that everything had to be connected to something else by a special wire cable and each cable could only fit into a particular plug and everything had to be done very carefully in exactly the right order.

Matt hesitated as he tried to find where the adapter attached. "Our equipment at Preston isn't nearly this complicated," he explained. "There seem to be a lot more choices to make."

Matt continued to plug and unplug different cables. After everything was together and working, it all seemed very logical.

Erin concentrated on every move as Matt began to take each thing apart. But by the time he was finished and the cables were lying in a twisted heap on the floor, she had forgotten the first step.

She struggled to attach the camera firmly to the tripod. *If this falls over, I'm finished,* Erin thought to herself. She tightened everything that seemed loose, then looked hopelessly down at the snaking wires at her feet, picking up one.

"Is this the camera cable?" she asked timidly, wishing that Matt wasn't standing there watching her confusion.

"No, the thick one. You've got the audio cable," he reminded her.

"Oh, of course. I remember now," she said. "The one with lots of prongs." She picked up the largest cable and began to plug it into the camera.

"Be careful. Don't force it," he warned. "It should just ease right in—then tighten it up."

"It must be the other end," Erin said as she noticed that the configuration of prongs didn't match the available holes.

"Here, let me help," Matt said.

He reached over and pushed the plug into place with a slight turn. "Okay. Now you attach the other end to the VCR."

Erin knelt down on the floor and examined the deck. Looking at the top as it stood on end, there were several possibilities, holes of various sizes and shapes, but none quite right. She started ripping open the various velcro flaps on the case searching for the hidden connection.

"Aha! I think I've found it," she exclaimed at last. "But this stupid canvas case is in the way. I can't get it in."

Matt came to the rescue again, deftly fitting the cable into the appropriate socket.

"Now let's see—What's next?" she asked herself out loud, still a little nervous. "How about the monitor? Now that will take this BLT cable here," she said, proudly picking up the right one.

Someone in the next group started to laugh, and Erin's face reddened. She looked at Matt questioningly.

"You're right," he said with a grin. "But it's BNC, not BLT."

"Oops!"

"Don't worry. They're probably not doing any better. You'll get it eventually."

Erin wasn't so sure. Even if she got everything together, it still might not work. It would be impossible to tell where she had made her mistake. It either worked or it didn't, and if it didn't she would have to start from the beginning again, checking every connection. This was *not* fun at all.

Erin looked at her watch, hoping it was time to go home.

"Okay, everybody," Eve called out from her perch on the light platform. "I know it's getting late, but I can't let you off the hook. You each have to put it together once. The more you do it, the easier it will be to remember."

Erin's heart sank. She had never in her whole life felt so stupid. She wondered if she would ever get it. What had made her think she had any talent for video, anyway? She didn't know the first thing about it. And this was only step one!

47

Reluctantly, she started tightening each connection, carefully going over each step in her mind. Finally she turned on each piece of equipment, starting with the adapter and ending with the monitor. There it was! A picture on the screen. It worked!

"Hey, you did it, Erin. Focus the camera and you're all set," Matt said encouragingly.

Cautiously she looked through the viewfinder and adjusted the focus. She zoomed in on Leslie across the room struggling to get her camera to fit back into the case. Then she panned the studio and noticed that just about everyone was having trouble with the unfamiliar tasks. *It wasn't just me*, she thought, relieved.

She felt much better now. Taking the stuff apart had to be easier than putting it together. But still there was a lot to remember. She had to close down the lens and put the cap back on, turn everything off in the right order, remove the microphone batteries, and eject the tape *before* she turned off all the power. She never seemed to be able to remember to do that.

When she finally got everything back where it belonged, her skin was damp with sweat and she was exhausted.

"What a workout!" she exclaimed to the world in general. "How'd you do?" she asked Jeff as he walked by on his way to the equipment closet.

"Oh, not too bad. Not too bad," he said.

"Come on, admit it was hard, Mr. Macho," Erin said.

"Sure, it was hard. But I think I can handle it," he answered confidently.

"Well, I don't know about you, but my brain feels like pea soup right now. I think it needs a nice long rest before I attempt any homework—like a couple of hours vegetating in front of junk TV. I think some game shows would do the trick."

"How about going next door with Leslie and me for some ice cream instead?" Jeff suggested. "That should make you feel human again."

"Sounds good to me. I'll see if Matt wants to come."

"Sure I'll go," Matt said when she asked. "I've been starving to death for the last hour."

Erin introduced him to Leslie and Jeff, and the four of them settled into a booth at Jerry's Ice Cream Shoppe.

"Erin tells us you're an expert," Leslie said to Matt as she dug into her tangerine sherbet.

"Not exactly," Matt answered. "I took a video course at Preston last year, but their equipment is pretty primitive compared to that at the studio here."

"Anyone who knows how to get the camera working as fast as you do looks like an expert to me," Erin said. "I have the feeling it's going to take me awhile to get the hang of it. There's so much to remember!"

"Once you've done it a few times it becomes automatic," Matt said.

"If you say so," Erin said, wanting to change the subject. "Tell us how you made your skateboarding tape. I've been telling these guys how great it is."

Matt flushed. "Well, it's not *Star Wars* or anything, but I got the idea from some of the kids in my neighborhood. They all have skateboards and have contests on the weekend. So I decided to follow them around with the camera, do a few interviews with them about how to get started, then go along to one of the competitions."

Matt described his adventures while Erin and her friends listened. They asked a million questions, and Matt regaled them with humorous stories of near disasters. By the time everyone had finished their ice cream they were laughing and chatting with Matt as if they had known him forever.

Eventually the conversation turned to their upcoming assignment.

"Does anybody have any ideas for the first project?" Leslie wondered. "It says here on the assignment sheet we're supposed to come in on Thursday with a list of ideas for four-minute spots."

"That sounds pretty easy," said Jeff. "Four minutes is no time at all."

"What do you think would be good, Matt?" Leslie asked.

"Interviews are pretty easy. You just ask a bunch of people what they think about something and edit all the answers together. Or a little feature on how to make something would be fun."

"How about a movie review?" Erin asked. "We could spend the weekend going to movies then tell which ones were good."

"I don't think that would be interesting without clips from the movies," said Jeff. "You've got to have some action to get people interested."

"I guess so," Erin said. "Anyway, we have a few more days to think about it."

Leslie and Jeff got up to clear their dishes

from the table while Matt and Erin lingered over their Cokes.

"I wanted to ask you something," Matt said. "If you haven't already promised someone else, would you be my partner for the project?"

Erin looked up, surprised. "You don't want to be tied down with a total beginner like me, do you?" she asked, hoping desperately that he did. "I wouldn't want to slow you down."

"Don't worry. I'll take my chances. I have a feeling you'll do just as well as those other jokers there."

She breathed a sigh of relief. Evidently she had not totally disgraced herself that day.

"Partners?" Matt asked, standing up and holding out his hand.

"Partners," Erin agreed, feeling the warmth of his hand closing over hers.

"Are you two coming?" asked Leslie, a knowing smile on her face.

Erin blushed and quickly dropped Matt's hand. But Matt didn't seem to mind. As they walked out of the booth, his hand rested lightly on the back of her neck.

"See you guys soon," Matt said when they caught up to Jeff and Leslie. "And, Erin, if you get any good ideas before Thursday, give me a call, okay?"

"Sure." She could hardly believe it. Matt still wanted to work with her. She had been afraid that he would look for a partner who caught on a little more quickly. Now she'd have a chance to show him that she had a lot of good ideas even if she didn't know VCR from VHS or BNC from BLT. Most of all, now she'd have a chance to spend more time with Matt Blakeslee.

Chapter Five

The house was unusually quiet when Erin arrived home from the studio. She decided it was a good time for her to do some thinking. Going up to her room, she settled into her favorite spot on the floor—right under the skylight that flooded the corner with the warm late-afternoon sun. She piled up her navy-and red-striped pillows under her head and stared up into the sky as tufts of clouds floated past.

She felt confused. The day before she had been on top of the world—full of confidence, ready to tackle anything. Now, after an hour of wrestling with cables and cords, she felt completely deflated. Would she ever be able to get a camera working by herself? She'd be lucky if she could find the outlets.

Her thoughts turned to Matt. He really knew his stuff. Maybe he wasn't an expert, but he was miles ahead of her. And for how long would he be willing to patiently explain things? She'd just have to catch up.

Then she let her imagination run wild. Matt and Erin, the famous documentary duo, traveling to exotic places to get their story— speaking with Barbara Walters in an elegant Manhattan apartment filled with souvenirs of their travels. . . . "Yes, Barbara, it all started when we were video students at New England Cable—we worked together on everything. . . ."

"Erin! Are you up there?" her mother called. "Dinner will be ready in a few minutes. Tell Davy it's time to set the table now."

"Okay, Mom."

After dinner Erin and her father cleared the table while Davy loaded the dishwasher. She told them about her first experience with the portable camera equipment that after- noon and asked for ideas for her four-minute spot.

As she expected, Davy sprang to life. "A music video!" he shouted. "I've got just the one. I'll need green hair spray, but it'll look great!"

"Thanks, but, no thanks, kid. My partner and I never work with child stars."

"Aw, come on."

"Let me know if you get some other ideas, though," Erin said, unable to resist his enthusiasm. "I might be able to use some of them."

The kitchen was quiet except for the clatter of dishes and silverware as they all tried to think of ideas. When Mrs. Marksson joined them, everyone was lost in thought.

"Why so quiet all of a sudden?"

"Shhhhh," Davy whispered. "We're having a think tank."

"Oh, I see. Well someone had better clue me in, too. I might be able to help," Mrs. Marksson said.

Erin explained her assignment to her mother, and they all sat down at the kitchen table and made a list of everything that came to mind, no matter how crazy or impossible it sounded. Then they went over the list and discussed each possibility.

An hour later Erin was still stuck. She had hoped to be able to call Matt with a dynamite idea, but none of the ones they had thought of so far seemed quite right. She'd have to keep thinking.

"Well, thanks for all the help, everybody. I guess I'll just have to solve this by myself," Erin said.

She settled down by the hall phone and dialed Leslie's number.

"Hi, Leslie. I was wondering how your video assignment was coming. Got any good ideas yet?"

"No, we haven't," Leslie answered a little tensely. "But we have a whole bunch of stupid ideas."

"Stupid! Who says they're stupid?" Jeff's voice carried over the phone.

"Jeff's over here now, and we're trying to find something we can both agree on," Leslie explained. "Would you believe he wanted to do an interview with the hockey coach? You know they'd never even let me into the locker room."

"How about this, Erin?" Jeff said, taking hold of the phone. "Do you think anyone in our video class would be interested in seeing Leslie's little sister's recorder recital? No way!"

"Katie *happens* to be very talented, and I think it would make a very interesting short video," Leslie said, regaining control of the phone.

"But that wasn't her worst idea," Jeff said, leaning close to the receiver as he spoke. "She wanted to explain pasta. You know, linguini, ziti, tortellini. Now, I like spaghetti as well as the next guy—but a video on pasta? I can see it now. Zoom in on that noodle!"

"You don't have to make fun of it," Leslie retorted. "There *are* people who are interested in food, you know."

Erin suppressed a giggle. "Well, it looks like you guys aren't going to be much help. I was hoping you'd have a few spare ideas that you wouldn't mind sending my way. My whole family has been working on this, and we haven't come up with a thing."

"Mom, where's the rabbit food?" Davy shouted. "I think I should feed Bugs and Nosey now."

"Please don't shout. I'm on the phone," Erin said, covering the receiver with her hand.

"Erin, I didn't know you had rabbits. When did you get them?" Leslie asked.

"Oh, my dad brought them home a couple of weeks ago. He was inspecting a development site out near the turnpike where the bulldozer operator had unearthed a nest of baby rabbits. They looked almost old enough to survive on their own, so my dad offered to bring them home for Davy."

"Where do you keep them?" Leslie asked.

"Outside in a little hutch next to the shed. You should come over and see them. They're awfully cute."

"You sure have some unusual pets in your neighborhood. Nothing simple like cats or dogs for you guys," Leslie said.

"What do you mean?"

"Don't you remember my sister Jenny's pet skunk?" Jeff chimed in. "We had to get it deperfumed, or whatever you call it, but after that it was as gentle as a kitten. We don't have it anymore, though."

"The Reilly garage isn't exactly my idea of a natural habitat," Leslie added.

"No, after a while we decided Stripes would be happier outdoors, so we gave him to the Wildlife Center. But it was sort of fun while we had him. Learned a lot about skunks—"

"I just got an idea," interrupted Leslie. "Why

don't you do a show on caring for wild pets? You could start with Davy's rabbits."

"Hey, that's not a bad idea at all—"

"Well, what are friends for, right? Just let me know when you come up with a good one for us, okay?"

"There's just one problem, though," Erin said with a sigh.

"What's that?"

"I don't think I'll be able to get away with taping Davy's pets without letting him in on it, too."

"I'll let you work on that problem," Leslie said, laughing. "I've got to hang up now. We've still got other homework to do over here."

No sooner had Erin hung up the phone than Davy was standing in front of her, nearly hopping with excitement.

"Did I hear you talking about doing your video on my rabbits?" he asked, trying to sound casual.

"Maybe you did, if you listen in on other people's conversations," Erin said, a little annoyed that he knew about the idea before she'd even had a chance to think it over.

"Then I can be in it?" he asked. "Someone has to hold them, and they like me best."

60

"I'll have to think about it. It just might be a terrific idea, but I'm not making any promises yet. I have to check everything with Matt first, you know."

"He's going to love it," Davy said confidently. "Right, Dad?"

"Sounds like a good idea to me. Oh, Erin, I just thought of something. One of the women at the office has a pet blue jay. It fell out of its nest last spring, and she fed it with an eye dropper and nursed it back to health. Now it's not afraid of her at all. Comes down and sits on her shoulder and eats out of her hand."

"Gee, do you think we could tape her, too?" Erin asked, starting to get excited.

"I'm sure she'd agree. She loves to tell the story of how she stayed up with it all the first night till she was sure it would make it."

Erin went up to her room and settled back down under the skylight. She couldn't decide whether or not to call Matt. He *had* said to call if she got any good ideas. But maybe this idea wasn't good enough. He might not like it, especially when he found out Davy was involved. If only he would call her first!

Leaning back onto the pillows and gazing

up through the skylight, she saw faint stars beginning to gleam through the dark evening sky. She wondered what Matt was doing then, if his mother was still working on her newsletter; if his dad was home; if he was sprawled in front of the TV with Tim or up in his room thinking about their project.

She couldn't wait any longer. Next to her phone was a small leather address book. She opened it to B, where she'd already written his name and number, followed by a string of tiny hearts.

The phone rang only twice after she dialed— then she heard his voice.

"Hi, Matt. This is Erin. Are you busy?" Why was her heart pounding?

"Not really," he said. "Just with homework, but I'm ready for a break."

"Have you thought of any ideas yet? For our video?"

"No," he admitted. "I haven't come up with a thing. My mind's been a total blank."

"Well, I've had my entire family brainstorming. Want to hear what we came up with?"

Matt's voice was amused. "Mostly I want to hear what Davy came up with. *Commando Raid in the Driveway*?"

"Close." Erin read him the list, including the pet idea, without hinting at which one she liked best.

"Wow! What a list. Next time I have a difficult assignment I think I'll come over to your house. I can't drum up any enthusiasm for my homework over here. Ever since my sister went away to college, I've been on my own."

"Which one do you like best?" Erin asked.

"Hmmm. Could you read them again?"

She ran through the list one more time.

"Davy's music video is tempting," Matt said with a laugh. "But I think the one about wild pets would be sort of fun, don't you?"

"That's the one I liked best, too," Erin said, relieved and a little amazed that they both agreed.

"But do you know anyone with wild pets?" Matt asked. "We have raccoons in the woods out behind the house, but they're not tame enough to be called pets."

Erin told him about Davy's wild rabbits and the woman with the blue jay.

Matt whistled in appreciation. "Looks like we're all set, then. I knew choosing you for a partner was a good idea. We're going to make a terrific team."

"We've got definite possibilities," Erin said with a smile.

They hung up soon after when Matt's father needed to use the phone. Erin settled back on her pillows, feeling as if she were glowing. Just talking to Matt made her happy. She felt like the luckiest girl in the world.

She sat down at her desk to start the rest of her homework, but she couldn't concentrate on anything except her video and Matt Blakeslee. Every few minutes she would jump up to add something to the growing list in her video notebook by the bed. She wished she could call Matt again but didn't want to risk getting him in trouble with his father by tying up their phone. Too bad it wasn't her night for aerobics at the Y, she mused. She felt like jumping and running and whirling around till she dropped.

That Thursday at the studio Matt and Erin started writing the script for their video. They began very seriously, deciding where they would shoot first and what scenes they wanted, then coming up with a series of questions about the rabbits and the blue jay, but the script soon degenerated. Maybe it was because they were trying to be too serious. Erin found herself writing a question that read, "In general, would you recommend keeping blue jays as pets?" And Matt scrawled the answer beneath it, "Only if they brush their teeth after meals."

"All right, so it wasn't the greatest question," Erin said, trying to keep a straight face.

Matt grinned. "Actually, it's not much worse than this one." He pointed to one of his own.

"What do you do with your blue jay?" Erin read in disbelief.

Matt flushed. "Well, I've never had a bird—I mean, what do you do when—"

Suddenly all of it seemed absurd, and they were laughing so hard that half the class turned to stare at them. Eve's glare sobered them up, and they decided to give the script a rest and spend some time practicing with the camera. Finally they reserved the equipment they would need for the weekend when they'd shoot the video.

By the time Erin went home that evening she was sure of two things. The first was that she had put together the equipment so often that she was positive she could do it in her sleep. The second was that she had never had so much fun with anyone as she had had with Matt Blakeslee.

It was nearly lunchtime on Friday before Erin realized that she hadn't spoken to Leslie in a while. And now her friend was nowhere to be found. Erin went into the cafeteria, got a tray of macaroni surprise, and finally saw Leslie in a far corner, sitting alone.

"Hey," she called out as she made her way over to the table. "How come you didn't wait for me?"

"You were late," Leslie answered glumly as Erin put down her tray.

"Well, here I am. And guess what? Matt and I decided to use your idea. We're going to film it on Saturday. Oh, Les, it's going to be so much fun!" Erin went on about her plans as Leslie stared vacantly across the room. "What do you think?" she asked when she had finished describing the closing scene they had come up with.

"What? About what?"

"Leslie, you haven't heard a word I've said. What's the matter with you, anyway?"

Leslie shook her head. "Oh, Erin. I had a

big fight with Jeff yesterday. Over the video. We both lost our tempers."

Erin felt a little embarrassed. She had been so involved with Matt and her project, she hadn't even noticed that her friend was hurting.

"I'm sorry, Les. Do you want to talk about it?"

"It was awful. I wish we'd never decided to work together." Leslie's dark eyes were beginning to fill with tears. "He was being such a know-it-all, I couldn't stand it anymore. I finally told him off, and now he's mad."

Erin knew that both Jeff and Leslie had hot tempers, but they had been going out for more than a year now. She couldn't believe their falling-out would last. "Why don't you call him up and talk it over?" she suggested. "He's probably just too proud to apologize."

"I don't think so. He's really mad. This time I think we're splitting for good. He even broke our date for Saturday night, and we've been planning to go to that concert for weeks. He'd already paid for the tickets!"

"That *is* serious!"

"I don't get it," Leslie said. "We're supposed to be partners, but Jeff thinks 'partners' means he's the boss and gets to decide everything. He expects me to agree with everything he says. Probably at our shoot he'll expect me to just tag along to hand him stuff, and—" Leslie couldn't go on. She buried her head in her arms.

"Oh, Les—" Erin put an arm around her friend's shoulders. It wasn't fair. Just as she and Matt were getting together, Jeff and Leslie were splitting up. She wished there was some way she could help.

Chapter Six

On Saturday Erin woke up as the early-morning light filtered through the yellowing maple leaves outside her skylight and into her bedroom. This was the big day: her first shoot with Matt. She had set her alarm for seven, but it hadn't gone off yet, and the house was still quiet. It was too early for anyone to be up and around on a Saturday.

She turned over to face the wall, determined to get another hour's sleep, but she was too excited. She kept going over their plans in her mind, trying to remember every detail.

As the sun rose higher in the sky, Erin's room became flooded with light that reflected off the white walls and the shiny white sur-faces of her desk and dresser. A cool breeze gently rang the wind chimes near her open window and twirled the red and yellow trian-gles of the mobile dangling over her bed. She pulled the flowered comforter up around her shoulders.

But when Davy's radio began to blare mu-sic into the upstairs hall, she knew she would never get back to sleep. He liked to get up early and get in a full morning of cartoons before the day's activities began.

She jumped out of bed and neatly smoothed out the sheets and covers, propping up her stuffed animal collection along the foot of the bed. They were starting to crowd her out, but she couldn't bear to banish any of them to the closet—much less throw them away—no matter how old and scruffy they looked.

Erin was a morning person. She always woke up full of energy and anxious to get started—even on a normal day. But that day she was a whirlwind. She showered, dried her hair, put on a pair of pink overalls and a white cotton turtleneck, and was in the mid-dle of trying out some pearly blue eye shadow before her mother called up to announce that breakfast was ready.

Halfway through breakfast the phone rang. Erin leapt up. "It's Matt! Let me get it."

"No, I want to," said Davy, who proved to be faster. "It's for me," he said smugly.

"Yippee!" he shouted, his face breaking into an excited smile. "Mommy," he called back to the kitchen. "It's Ben. His father got some tickets to the Red Sox game this afternoon, and they want to know if I can go. Can I?"

"Don't you dare even think about going to that game, David Marksson," Erin said, interrupting. "You promised to be in my video today, and you can't change your mind now."

"Oh, Erin." Davy looked upset. "I've *got* to go to this game."

"I thought you wanted to be on TV," Erin said, trying not to feel sorry for him.

"I do! I want to do both! Couldn't you change your shoot? Please?" Davy looked at her hopefully.

"I really can't. All I can promise is that we'll do it as quickly as possible," she said, giving in a little. "Maybe we'll be done in time."

"But they want to know *now*. If I can't come they're going to give the ticket to someone else," Davy said, whining.

"But, Davy, I really don't know how long it's going to take. If we make a lot of mistakes, we might have to do it over a couple of times."

Mrs. Marksson stepped in before the argument got out of hand. "You're going to have to stick with your commitment to Erin, Davy. You begged to be in her show, and now she's counting on you. There'll be other games."

"No, there won't. It's the end of the season. This'll be the last one I'll get to see."

"Well, Davy, you did promise. And if you back out now, Erin probably won't give you another chance," Mrs. Marksson stated.

"I guess you're right," Davy admitted. "And this might be my only chance to be on TV."

Ben was impressed and offered to miss the game himself if he could be in the video, too, but Erin said one seven-year-old was plenty.

When Erin heard the crunch of gravel, she raced up the stairs to her room.

"Mom, get the door, okay? I'll be there in a minute," she called down.

Erin had decided that she didn't like the blue eye shadow after all. She rushed to her room and started rubbing at her eye until only the faintest hint of blue remained.

She didn't want to look too feminine that day, she decided. This was a workday, and she wanted Matt to know she could do the job—any job that needed to be done. Because of her small frame and delicate good looks, people sometimes underestimated Erin's capabilities. They frequently offered to do things for her that she was perfectly capable of doing herself. She definitely didn't want Matt to think of her as delicate and frail. *Maybe these pink overalls are too . . . No, never mind,* she thought to herself. Pink *was* her favorite color; she couldn't change that.

Satisfied that she looked her best, she went downstairs to find Matt sitting at the kitchen table, coaching Davy on how to act during his interview.

"Okay, now, I want you to practice your part with this cassette recorder while we're getting the equipment," he said seriously. "Get it nice and smooth, okay?"

He looked up as she walked in, and a smile lit up his face. "Come on, Erin, let's go. If we don't get everything checked out by ten o'clock, the staff will be busy and we'll be out of luck."

"I'm ready," she said, thinking how good it was to see him sitting there in her kitchen. "Let's go."

They quickly drove the few blocks to the studio and parked near the loading ramp in back. Once inside they got out their list of equipment. After several trips into the large storeroom they had an incredible pile in front of them on the floor. They put it all together to make sure everything was working properly, then had to take it all apart for the trip to Erin's house.

Finally Erin got some tapes and began signing out the equipment.

"Here, let me take some of this heavy stuff, too. I'm stronger than I look," she said to Matt who was already loading the equipment into the car.

"If you say so. Here's the camera," he said, handing her the case.

She gamely lugged it down the ramp and came back for another load.

"Well, that's it," Matt said after a few more trips.

He banged the trunk closed. "You got those tapes, didn't you?"

"Yeah, I got them, but I'm not sure what I did with them. Check the pockets of the camera case."

"Nope, not here." Matt looked a little impatient.

"The bag with the extension cords?"

"No. They're not in the trunk at all."

"I know," Erin said, remembering at last. "I must have left them on the table when I was filling in the sign-out sheet." She quickly ran back up to the studio, retrieved the missing tapes, and climbed into the front seat, relieved that she had found them.

Erin hoped she could keep her mind on the work. Right then, sitting next to Matt, she was more aware of his strong hands on the wheel and his dark eyes that turned to look at her from time to time as he navigated the busy Ashboro streets. She found herself wishing they were on their way to the Cape, with picnic baskets and beach towels piled up behind them instead of cameras and lights. She'd much rather be lying beside Matt on the hot sand than struggling to remember which buttons to push and trying to make her nutty brother act like a reasonably normal person.

Back at Erin's house, they quickly unloaded the Saab and started to set up in the little porch at the back of the house.

Amazingly Erin remembered where everything went. She connected the adapter to the deck and the deck to the monitor and the camera, then began to turn each piece on. Everything was fine until the last step.

"I can't get the camera to work," she said nervously. "The power is on, but I can't see anything."

Matt grinned. "You have to have a tape in for the camera to work. Remember?"

"Oh, yeah," she said as she reached for a tape and slipped it into the deck.

"Call Davy, and we'll test his voice level on the microphone," Matt said, taking the tiny lavalier mike from its box.

When Erin returned with Davy, who was carefully carrying Bugs and Nosey, one in each hand, Matt looked annoyed. Erin looked around anxiously, wondering what had happened.

"You know we tested the mike this morning?" he said. "Well, someone left it turned on, and now the battery is dead."

"I guess that someone was me," Erin admitted sheepishly. "Sorry, Matt. I forgot to take out the battery."

"We're going to be here all day at this rate," he said a little sharply.

Erin felt devastated.

"I'm sorry," she mumbled awkwardly.

Matt glared at her for a long moment. Then she saw the old smile return.

"Never mind," he said. "It must have been

practically dead, anyway, to go in that short a time. Don't worry about it. At least it died before we got started shooting."

He stepped over to her, put an arm around her slumped shoulders, and gave her a little hug. "Cheer up, Erin," he said softly. "These things happen to everybody. You'll just know better next time."

"I guess so," she answered glumly.

"I should've brought some extras, anyway. It's always good to have a spare."

Erin stared at the floor, unable to respond.

"Well, Davy can squeeze in a few more cartoons before we get going," Matt said. "It'll just take a minute for me to run back and get some new batteries. Erin, turn all this stuff off and set up the lights while I'm gone, okay?"

Davy raced off to the TV room to catch the end of his favorite Saturday-morning cartoon, and Erin began setting up the tripods for the lights, placing one on each side of the area where they were planning to shoot. When she turned them on, the usually shady back porch was flooded with light.

At least these are working okay, she told herself as she turned them off again. *But what else can go wrong?*

*   *   *

Twenty minutes later Matt returned with a packet of new batteries for the mike. Davy went through his lines one more time, and everything seemed ready at last.

"This is it, folks. Everything's plugged in. The adapter is—on," Matt said as he pushed its power button. "The deck is—on," he said, continuing. "And the monitor. Now the camera. Erin, get the lights."

She reached up and turned on the first one.

"Do you think one is enough?" she asked. "It's pretty bright."

"No, point the second one up at the ceiling. That'll give us a little backlighting," Matt said.

Erin aimed the second light up at a point just beyond where Davy was standing and flipped the switch. The porch lit up for one second—then everything went black.

"Did you plug everything into the same outlet?" Matt asked, barely disguising his annoyance at this final setback. "You *know* those lights draw a lot of power. You have to use at *least* two different circuits."

"Not again," said Davy. "Do I have the world's dumbest sister, or what?"

"Creep," Erin hissed as she made a lunge

for her brother's ear, but Davy expertly dodged her grasp and made a quick exit.

Erin felt humiliated. Furtively, she wiped her eyes that were slowly filling with tears. Davy was right. She was too dumb for this. She couldn't even bring herself to look at Matt.

Matt pulled a mini flashlight from one of his pockets, then turned all the equipment off so the circuit wouldn't blow again when the power came back on.

"Luckily, 'Be prepared' is my motto," he said, flourishing the flashlight. "Just show me where the basement is, and I'll reset the circuit breaker."

Matt took Erin's hand, and they found their way down to the electric box in a dark corner of the basement. As they stood next to each other, he gave her hand a squeeze.

"I'm sorry I got mad. Everyone makes mistakes, and I've made plenty myself, that's for sure."

Erin looked up from her scuffed white sneakers, but she didn't know what to say. She wished she could make a promise to do better, but she wasn't sure she'd be able to keep it.

"Cheer up," Matt said gently. "We've got work to do."

Erin tried to look more cheerful than she felt as the lights came back on.

"Okay, Davy, we're definitely ready to roll," Matt called out as they ran back up the basement stairs. Davy came in carrying the rabbits again, and Erin quickly attached the microphone to his collar and picked up the hand-held mike herself. At last, everything was working.

"Today we have seven-year-old Davy Marksson with us. Davy is caring for two wild rabbits whose nest was destroyed in a construction project. Tell us how you got your pets, Davy," Erin began.

Davy began confidently, telling how his father had brought the bunnies home in an old Happy Meal box as Matt went from a wide shot of Erin and Davy to a close-up of the bunnies.

"And how did you find out how to care for young rabbits?" Erin continued.

"Well, we called the Wildlife Center where they take care of animals that are injured or sick, and they can tell you how to care for baby animals if you don't know what to feed them."

Davy set Bugs down on the table and offered him a large leaf of lettuce as Matt zoomed in closer.

"Do you think rabbits make good pets?" Erin asked, smiling at her brother.

"Yes, I think rabbits make very good pets," he said authoritatively. "If you can't find a wild one, which you probably can't because they run real fast, I think you can buy them at a store. The only thing is they might be white, and the white ones have pink eyes, which I think is ugly, but otherwise they're pretty much the same."

"In closing, do you have any advice for our viewers?" Erin asked. Matt pulled up to focus on Davy as they wrapped it up.

"Just one thing. If you take your pet out of its cage to play with it, you better be inside or have a fence, because he might try to run away. This happened to me, once. I called his name, but he didn't come back and I almost didn't catch him. So my advice is be careful!"

"Thank you very much for sharing Bugs and Nosey with us today," Erin said, beginning the wrap-up. "If any of you viewers have questions about wild animals, call the Wildlife Center. They are equipped to help you."

She turned the mike off and shot Matt a look of pure relief.

"That went pretty well," he said. "Don't anybody leave yet, though. I need a few more shots of the rabbits and you two."

He shot a few more minutes of the rabbits eating the lettuce and hopping and a couple of Erin nodding and smiling as if she were listening to Davy's comments. They would use these in the editing to cover any places where Matt had jiggled the camera or gotten out of focus.

"Do you think the extension cord is long enough to show the hutches out in back?" Erin asked. "That would make a nice opening shot."

"That's a good idea, let's give it a try," Matt said.

Half an hour later the equipment was packed up and loaded into the car, and Erin and Matt were relaxing in the kitchen with cold sodas.

"Do we really have to do the blue jay today?" Erin asked, unable to face the thought of starting all over again.

"This *has* been a little rough. I'll call the studio and see if we can keep the camera out one more day."

As Matt made the call, Erin promised herself that next time she would do better. At least he wasn't angry with her anymore. It was all right to make mistakes occasionally, but enough was enough. Even someone with the patience of a saint would get angry eventually if she kept screwing up. The next day she would have everything completely under control.

Mrs. Levine had asked them to be there at ten o'clock sharp on Sunday, so Erin was ready and waiting at nine-thirty, determined not to be the cause of any more problems. It was a beautiful fall day, just cool enough to make her want to put away her tank tops for good and turn to wool sweaters and plaid flannel shirts. As she waited impatiently for Matt, she heard the sound of birds just outside the window. She looked out and saw hundreds of fluttering dark shapes, probably starlings, among the brilliant yellow leaves of her maple tree, a traditional gathering place for the birds who passed through Boston to go south every year.

Suddenly she had a terrible thought. There *was* something that could go wrong. The bird might attempt to fly south. She could just imagine it winging off in the middle of the video. Worse, it could have already taken off.

It was a relief when they pulled into Mrs. Levine's driveway, and she came out to greet them with the young blue-jay perched on her shoulder.

This time it was Erin's turn to operate the camera while Matt asked the questions. They set up on the patio so they could use natural light and ran an extension cord inside to a plug. They were able to set up quickly and had only one near miss—Erin had to be reminded to use the outdoor filter on the camera.

Mrs. Levine explained how the bird had fallen from its nest in the big oak tree next to her house and how she was told to feed it little gobs of cat food on the eraser end of a pencil every twenty minutes, from dawn to dusk, for three weeks.

"Can you imagine that?" she exclaimed. "My husband thought I was crazy, but he and my daughter, Deborah, both helped."

Erin followed the bird as the woman talked, trying to keep it in focus as it perched on her shoulder, then her head, then flew down to peck at some birdseed.

"You know, little Jay-Jay is so smart," she

said. "When I come out to work in the garden, he flies down and sits on the brim of my straw hat as I work, and he just has a feast with all the bugs and worms I turn up while weeding."

"Let's try to get a shot of that," Erin suggested.

They stopped while Mrs. Levine went inside to get her hat and gardening gloves, then moved the equipment over to the flower bed to get Jay-Jay in action. Then it was back to the patio for a few final questions by Matt.

Erin breathed a sigh of relief as the interview came to a close. She had expected disaster at every step and still couldn't believe there had been no major mishaps. It had been exhausting, though. Her head was pounding from the tension of trying to do everything perfectly. And her stomach was in no condition to accept the Danish and tea that Mrs. Levine was urging them to eat.

Chapter Seven

When Matt dropped her off after the taping session, Erin was almost relieved that he had to go right home and help his parents with some yard work. She needed some time by herself.

"Did you blow the lights out again?" Davy asked as soon as she walked in the door.

"No, I did not, Mr. Wise Guy."

"Well, what did you do wrong this time, then?" he persisted.

"Nothing. I didn't do *anything* wrong this time. Come on, give me a break, Davy. I'm really tired."

"Did he kiss you yet?" Davy asked, grinning from behind the door.

"None of your business," Erin replied, throwing down her jacket and heading for the back door.

She felt like doing a little yard work herself. At least that way Davy wouldn't be hanging around asking embarrassing questions. When there was work to be done, he usually made himself scarce. She found a rake in the toolshed and began to rake the maple leaves from the big tree into a pile.

The leaves were just starting to fall. A thin layer of yellow covered most of the grass without diminishing the ceiling of leaves overhead. The yard didn't really need to be raked yet. More leaves would fall soon and the job would have to be redone, but the mindlessness of the task was relaxing. No chance for error.

After an hour Erin felt that she had made enough of a contribution, especially since a blister was developing on her right hand. As she started into the house to get some leaf bags, Leslie rode up the driveway on her bike.

"Hi, I've been trying to call you all afternoon. Someone must be having a pretty heavy conversation. Your line's been busy since noon."

"Well, it wasn't me. I've been out here raking leaves," Erin replied. "Be back in a second. I need to find some leaf bags before Davy starts jumping in these leaves and spreads them all over again."

Erin returned with the oversize bags and gave them to Leslie to hold open while she filled them.

"So what's up?" Erin asked. "What did you want to talk to me about?"

"I need your advice," Leslie confided. "About Jeff."

"Uh-oh. It's risky giving advice to the lovelorn. What if it doesn't work? Besides, Jeff might get mad at me for butting in."

"I promise, I won't blame you for anything. I just want to know what you would do in my place, that's all."

"Okay," Erin said. "But remember, whatever happens, it's not my fault."

"Right. Unless you tell me to do something *really* stupid."

"Leslie!"

"Just kidding. Just kidding."

The girls finished filling the bags and piled them up next to the toolshed.

"Let's ride over to the arboretum," Leslie suggested. "Then we can talk. I've been in the house trying to practice for my piano recital all day, and I'm dying for some fresh air."

"Okay," Erin agreed. "I haven't been out on my bike for ages." She wheeled her dusty Fuji out of the garage and immediately noticed it had two low tires. "Let's take a walk up to the gas station first. I need some air."

They walked along the sidewalk toward the main street, pushing their bikes ahead of them. As they passed the Reilly house, Leslie looked straight ahead but couldn't resist taking a few furtive glances in its direction to see if there was any sign of Jeff.

"His car's gone. He must be out with Mike and Roger," Erin said.

"I couldn't care less," her friend exclaimed, tossing her long black ponytail over her shoulder to emphasize her lack of interest.

This looks pretty serious, Erin thought to herself. She had never seen Leslie so upset.

"Well, which way should we go?" Erin asked after she had filled her tires at the air pump.

They decided on the river route and pedaled down to the bicycle path along the river. There they threaded past strollers and people in lawn chairs reading the Sunday papers. Long tendrils from the giant weeping willows that lined the bank hung over the path and brushed against their faces as they rode by.

"What are you doing for your project, anyway?" Erin asked.

"Nothing. That's the problem. We keep picking topics, work on them for a while, argue, then start over. We can't seem to get it together."

As their pace slowed on the last long hill before the entrance to the arboretum, Erin was glad she had a ten-speed. Before she got it, she had always had to walk the last few blocks.

"The first thing you have to promise is no more starting over," Erin said. "There just isn't enough time. Pick a topic and stick with it no matter what. At least you'll be making progress, even if you are still fighting a lot."

"I guess so. We've spent an awful lot of time writing scripts that ended up in the trash barrel," Leslie admitted.

They slipped in through the partially opened iron gate and headed toward the apple orchard. A few of the older trees had thick branches low enough for the girls to climb up and reach the apples that had not yet fallen to the ground. Nothing tasted better than an apple picked fresh from a tree.

The fruit had been pretty well picked over by the squirrels and the neighborhood kids, but a few big juicy ones remained near the top of the tree, and Leslie, who was taller, strained to reach them.

"Here, catch," she called down to Erin who was balancing in a lower fork of the tree. "I need both hands to get down."

Erin deftly caught them and stuck one in each pocket of her sweatshirt.

They sat quietly, propped in the tree, munching on their apples until Leslie broke the silence.

"I wish I'd never taken this video course," she said vehemently. "Jeff and I used to have so much fun together. But now that we're partners on this project, we're arguing all the time. I don't get it."

"Have you ever worked on something together before?" Erin asked.

"We always do our homework together. And I helped him with a couple of science experiments he had to make up, but that's about it."

"So what is it exactly that you argue about?"

"Everything," Leslie moaned. "What we're going to do, when, where, who's going to carry what—every detail. It's awful. I didn't know there were so many things two people could disagree about."

"How about if you divided the project into two parts with equal responsibilities. Each person would be the boss of his or her half, and you could flip a coin to see who got what."

"It might work—*if* we could agree on how to divide it. Unfortunately, we're not speaking at the moment. I think it would be easier to ask for a more agreeable partner."

"It would be. Except everyone already has a partner. You'd still have to straighten this out with Jeff, eventually. You can't just ignore each other forever."

"Believe me, I tried to explain my point of view. He actually hung up on me."

"Really?"

"And his sister told me he wasn't home the last time I called."

"Well, maybe he wasn't," Erin said, thinking that Jeff couldn't be *that* obstinate.

"I can't take it anymore. You've got to talk to him for me," Leslie pleaded, almost in tears.

Erin reluctantly agreed. She couldn't turn her friend down, although she had serious misgivings about her chances of success.

"Talk to him this evening, all right? Video class is tomorrow, and we've got to finish planning our project or we'll both flunk."

"I'll try," Erin said, wondering if Jeff could really be acting as awfully as Leslie claimed.

It was starting to cloud over, and the temperature was dropping, so they decided to head home. They coasted down the long hill that had been so hard to climb on the way over and raced along the river path in record time.

"Don't forget, now," Leslie called out as she turned onto her street. "I'm counting on you."

Erin continued on down Spring Street several more blocks before turning. She passed the Reillys' house once more, noting that Jeff's old heap was now in the driveway. Maybe she could think of an excuse to drop by after dinner. She wasn't looking forward to it though.

She kept pedaling until she reached her own house and saw Davy out in the front yard throwing his baseball up in the air and trying to catch it. He wasn't too successful.

"Would you play catch with me, Erin?" Davy asked as he followed her to the garage while she put her bike away. "When I throw it myself, I can't catch it too well."

"Okay," Erin said. "For a few minutes."

They tossed the ball back and forth while Erin thought about how to start her conversation with Jeff. Then she got an idea.

"Davy, I think Jeff's home now. Why don't

you run over and see if he wants to play, too. That would make a better game."

Jeff, the middle child in a family with four sisters, had taken Davy under his wing and was helping him perfect his pitching arm.

Davy ran over to the Reillys' and soon reappeared with Jeff, carrying a couple of fielder's mitts.

"Run back, Davy," Jeff called out. "I'll give you a high one."

The ball flew almost straight up, arching higher than the house, before descending directly over Davy and glancing off his outstretched glove.

"Oops. Guess I missed it," Davy admitted good-naturedly as he chased after the ball. "Here, get this one," he cried, throwing it so far to the side that Jeff nearly ran into a tree trying to make the catch.

Her mission accomplished, Erin quietly dropped out of the game and sat on the edge of the curb to wait for Jeff to take a break. Davy soon tired him out, and he sat down next to Erin to catch his breath.

"Boy, he's really something," Jeff said. "If I did this every afternoon, I'd be ready for hockey season in no time. Being a lifeguard all summer was great for my tan but not too good for keeping in shape."

"Don't worry, the coach'll have you running laps again soon," Erin said.

"No kidding . . . I hope all this video stuff doesn't keep me from getting in shape for hockey tryouts. It's not as much fun as it was in the beginning."

Erin was relieved that Jeff had brought up the subject himself. She hadn't figured out a way to get the conversation started.

"How's your project going?" she asked innocently.

"Terrible. We can't even plan it, much less finish it. Leslie insists on haggling over every single detail. I'm fed up. I just want to get the thing over with so I have time for my other stuff, and she wants to discuss everything to death. We'll never get it done in time at this rate."

"Why don't you agree to stop arguing at least?" Erin suggested. "You take charge of some things and let her take charge of some things and agree to go along with the other person's decisions, no matter what."

"That *sounds* good. But Leslie would never agree. She's such a perfectionist, she has to make sure every little thing is just the way she wants it," Jeff said, sounding discouraged.

"Well, you *could* give it a try. Why don't you

call her up and try to settle it? If one of you doesn't make a move soon, you'll never get it done."

"Okay, I'll give it a try," Jeff said doubtfully as he got up and headed back to his house. "Thanks for the advice. See you tomorrow."

Erin stood up and stretched, proud of herself for engineering a reconciliation, or what she hoped would be one. At least they would be talking to each other again, and that would be an improvement.

All in all, it had been a good day. She thought about how smoothly things had gone that morning with Matt as they shot the sequence on Mrs. Levine's blue jay—just like clockwork. They were turning out to be quite a team after all.

Chapter Eight

It was Monday, and the three friends were on their way over to the cable studio after school. Leslie and Jeff had called a truce, having agreed to try Erin's suggestion of dividing responsibility for the project, and they strolled together across the leaf-strewn lawn in front of Ashboro High.

"Do you mean to tell me that you and Matt never argue about your video?" Jeff asked.

"Well, we haven't had any problems yet," Erin said. "Of course, Matt has had more experience at this than I have, so I think I'd probably be willing to try things his way even if we disagreed."

"Hah! What did I tell you, Leslie? Matt makes the decisions, and our beautiful Erin here thinks that's cool."

"Just one difference," Leslie said, "Matt knows what he's doing and *you don't*."

"A matter of opinion."

"Yeah, and my opinion is just as good as your opinion," Leslie said, starting to get upset all over again.

"Wait a minute, wait a minute," Erin said, interrupting. "You two promised to quit fighting about this!"

They heard a car horn beeping behind them. As Erin turned, a blue Saab pulled up beside her.

"Matt!" she called out.

"Hop in, guys. I'll give you a lift." Erin slid in beside Matt while Jeff and Leslie jumped in back. "Thought I might pass you if I took this route," Matt said. "I couldn't wait to tell you that I took a look at the stuff we shot this weekend, and it's not bad. The camera was a little unsteady in a few spots, but I think we can edit those out pretty easily."

Erin breathed a sigh of relief. Nothing else had gone wrong.

While Matt looked straight ahead, concentrating on the heavy traffic around the high school, Erin took the opportunity to appreciate just how good-looking he was. His nose was straight, almost movie-star quality, but his mouth seemed a little crooked. Maybe it was because he always had a slightly amused look on his face. Nothing seemed to really bother him, and he could always make her laugh. Besides all of that, he was one of the nicest people she had ever met. How had she lucked into teaming up with him?

He glanced over and caught her eye, but she looked down quickly, hoping he hadn't noticed her examining every detail of his face. Matt reached over and put his hand over hers as he drove. His touch was warm on her cool fingers. She closed her eyes and sank back into the bucket seat hoping that moment would never end.

"Here we are," Matt said as he put both hands on the wheel to back into a tight parking space in front of the studio. "Leave your stuff in here if you want to, and I'll give you all a ride home later."

Erin gave Leslie a hard look.

"Oh that's okay. Jeff and I like to walk," Leslie answered before Jeff could accept the invitation. "You go ahead and take Erin."

Matt looked questioningly at Erin.

"I'd love a ride," she said. "My books weigh a ton today. I must have homework in every subject."

The afternoon went quickly as the interns discussed their work and started making plans for a second, longer video. Erin and Matt began a tentative editing script for the pet tape and tossed out a few ideas for their next project. Erin suggested the Multicultural Festival that was to be held at Ashboro High soon, and Matt suggested doing one on local fishing spots.

The class seemed to fly by, and before she knew it, it was time to help put away the equipment. The kids in the class made plans to go next door to Jerry's. By some sort of unspoken agreement, she and Matt lingered in the hall, reading the bulletin board as the others filed out.

When they finally got to the ice cream shop, the gang from the studio were about to leave. Erin was glad. She was tired of sharing Matt with the other kids, who all came to him for advice. Except for that first day when she had visited his house, they had never really been alone.

They both got chocolate chocolate-chip ice

cream with chocolate sauce and slipped into a booth in the back corner.

"Another chocolate freak," Matt said.

"Yeah, sometimes I get the urge to try some new flavors, but at the last minute I can't resist chocolate. Especially when I heard your order, I knew I wouldn't be satisfied with a wimpy lime sherbet," Erin said.

"Wimpy! That's my second favorite flavor," Matt said, laughing.

"Sorry. I guess it's not *too* bad."

"What's with Leslie and Jeff?" Matt asked, suddenly sounding serious. "They both seemed to be in pretty bad moods. Are they having trouble with their taping?"

"They've been arguing a lot. They both want to be the boss and do everything their own way. I tried to get them to compromise, but I'm not sure it's working. Leslie was getting pretty steamed again this afternoon."

"It *is* hard to do a project like this when you and your partner don't see eye to eye. At Preston, we didn't have to work in groups. Too many artistic egos involved. But here I like it. Especially when there's so much to remember; it's nice to have company."

"Mmm-hmm." Erin nodded, as she scooped

up the last of the chocolate sauce. She wondered if Matt had an "artistic ego."

"Well, we'd better figure out what we're doing next. Tell me more about the Multicultural Festival," Matt said.

"We have this one day each year when all the different ethnic groups in our school set up booths in the gym. They demonstrate crafts, sell snacks, wear national costumes, or think of some way to represent the culture of their native country. Then all evening there are demonstrations of music and dancing by semiprofessional groups from the area."

"Sounds colorful," Matt said. "But what do you think of the fishing idea?"

"Well, talking to the fishermen might be interesting, but fishing isn't a very visual event," she said honestly. "We could wait for hours without anyone catching more than an old tin can."

"You're probably right. Okay, let's go for the festival. There'll be plenty of action there. Just let me know the exact date, and I'll sign out the equipment we need," Matt said as he got up and cleared away his place. "I've got to get going now. I'll drop you off."

Erin got up, wishing they could stay and talk a little longer. They never seemed to have time for personal conversations. It was always shop talk. Still, it was better than nothing at all.

In a few minutes she was standing on the curb in front of her house waving as the blue Saab disappeared around the corner. *It might be better to have a boyfriend who didn't have his own car,* she thought for a moment as she stood staring at the spot where his car had disappeared. *If Matt walked me home, he couldn't rush off so fast.*

Erin still wasn't sure if Matt *liked* her—*really* liked her. He was very nice to her, he *seemed* interested in her, but did he feel as strongly as she did? She couldn't stand it when the other girls in the class crowded around asking him questions. She knew she was hooked.

Once inside, she went right up to her room and called Leslie. She needed a second opinion.

"Leslie," Erin said when her friend answered, "I have to ask you something important."

"Ask away."

"Do you think Matt really likes me, or do you think he's just being friendly because none of his friends from school are around? Now be honest."

"You're sure you want me to be completely honest?" Leslie asked in a testing voice.

"Absolutely. I have to know what you think." Erin closed her eyes, half expecting the worst.

"Well, of course. *I* think he's *crazy* about you. He picked you out the first day, and he's been following you around ever since. He wouldn't have chosen you for his partner unless he liked you—you're not exactly a video expert, you know."

"Please. Don't rub it in. You *know* I made a fool of myself on our first shoot."

"Well, that proves it. He gave you another chance because he likes you so much."

"Oh, I hope so. I've never liked anyone so much. Just sitting next to him makes my heart race. Do you feel that way about Jeff?"

"Well, not at the moment," Leslie said sourly. "But I know what you mean—it's like everything is more intense, more real somehow when you're with that person."

"Exactly. When I'm home I feel so bored and empty. I just count off the hours until I'll see him again."

"Well, I wouldn't worry," Leslie said, reassuring her. "The way he looks at you—it's got to be love."

"Are you sure you're not just saying that?" Erin couldn't help asking.

"Yes, I'm *sure*. Listen, I've got to hang up now. I have to spend some time at the piano before dinner. Talk to you tomorrow."

"Okay. 'Bye." Erin put down the phone and walked to her bedroom in a daze, hearing Leslie's words echo in her mind: "The way he looks at you—it's got to be love."

The next evening after dinner Matt picked Erin up and they drove over to the studio to take a look at the raw footage they had taped so far. They let themselves into the empty control room. Two chairs faced a panel of monitors mounted above rows of buttons and red and green indicator lights. As Erin experimentally flipped a few switches near the door, the lights went on and the air conditioner sprang into action.

Matt quickly set up the board for editing, making sure that everything was in working order, and put their tapes into the proper decks.

Once they were set up, Matt and Erin sat back to view their work and found that most of the tape with Davy and the bunnies was useable. After they had previewed all the raw footage, including the blue jay sequence, it took half an hour, using the trial-and-error method, to make the first edit. Luckily, things speeded up after that.

"You know, this is almost like magic," Erin exclaimed as she struggled to get the hang of it.

"Yeah, it's neat, isn't it?" he said. "What I like about it is you can always do something over. You can try something one way and if you don't like it you can do it again another way until you get it just the way you want it. Of course you can spend hours reworking everything, if you're picky like me. The main thing you have to remember is to concentrate. If your mind is somewhere else, you're bound to mess up."

Erin proved him right a moment later by thoughtlessly pressing the "program" button instead of "preview." She had to set up the edit all over again from the beginning. She had been thinking about Matt, of course, fantasizing again about their future as a famous video duo. Matt gave her a weary look but didn't say anything.

Two hours later they had edited four minutes and were ready to quit. Erin's fingers were icy in spite of the heavy wool sweater she had remembered to wear that evening.

"Hey, you're freezing, aren't you?" Matt said as his hand brushed against hers. "You should've said something."

"It's okay. I'm always a little cold," Erin said.

"Here, let me warm up those hands." Matt took her small hands in both of his and rubbed them gently.

The warmth of his touch melted away the tension that had been building up as they worked.

"I can't believe it took us two hours to do four minutes," Erin said with a sigh. "Does it usually take you that long?"

"Sometimes longer. It's better to work slowly and carefully than to have to go back and do a whole segment over again. I've found that out the hard way."

"I have a feeling that's how everything is learned around here," Erin said. "The hard way."

One of the technicians looked into the control room. "You guys done, I hope? We've got to lock up now. Bring your tapes up to the cabinet, and I'll shut everything off in here."

As they drove home, Erin felt the beginnings of what was now a familiar tug-of-war in her mind. There was nothing she wanted more than to spend time with Matt, and yet the idea of doing the second video with him scared her to death. She just couldn't bear any more mistakes that would make her look like an idiot in front of him.

"Have you warmed up yet?" Matt's words broke into her thoughts as they pulled up in front of her house.

"Almost."

He looked down at her, smiling. "I can't let you go home cold. Come here." And then he took her in his arms and held her close.

For a moment Erin forgot all about videos and making a fool of herself. All that mattered was how good it felt to be in Matt's arms.

Chapter Nine

The evening of the Multicultural Festival Erin felt rushed and very nervous.

"I want you to eat something before you go," Mrs. Marksson said. "You shouldn't go off for the evening on an empty stomach, Erin."

"But I'm not hungry, Mom. I really couldn't eat a thing right now. Besides, they're selling snacks at some of the booths. I'll get something later if I get hungry."

"Here's an apple. It might come in handy." Her mother slipped a large red apple into Erin's leather shoulder bag and gave her a quick kiss. "Good luck. And don't be too late."

"Right, Mom."

"Remember this *is* a school night."

"Here he is," Erin said as she saw Matt's car pull into the drive. " 'Bye, Mom."

She glanced into the backseat as she climbed in next to Matt. Just seeing the jumble of extension cords and cables gave her stomach a turn.

"Hey, don't look so worried," Matt said as he turned to back out of the drive. "Everything'll be fine."

"I'm just a little nervous," Erin explained.

"Nervous! You look like you're going in front of a firing squad. It can't be that bad. We'll take everything nice and slowly, and it'll go fine. You'll see."

They found a parking spot right near the side door and began hauling their equipment into the gym. Colorfully decorated craft booths lined the walls, and crepe-paper streamers fluttered from the corner poles.

They searched for electrical outlets, trying to find a spot where they could plug everything in but still get a good view of things and be out of the way of the crowds passing in front of the exhibits.

"How about over there next to the origami table," suggested Matt. "That way we can move

110

up this aisle and get shots of the booths on either side."

"Looks good to me," Erin agreed, pulling the cords between two exhibits and plugging them in behind the folded bleachers.

"Now, don't take this the wrong way, Erin, but you *did* plug the lights into a different socket from the camera and deck, didn't you?" Matt kidded.

"Of course I did. I never make the same mistake twice."

"Just checking."

"I try to find new ones," Erin said, trying to sound lighthearted. She knew Matt was teasing, but bringing up the last disaster made her even more nervous.

She struggled with the tripod for a few minutes, trying to get the legs even. It was different from the one they had had for their last taping session, and she had trouble attaching the camera. *It isn't fair,* she thought. *I get one thing figured out, and they switch everything on me!* Finally the camera slipped into place.

She clipped a lavaliere mike to her shirt, picked up the hand-held mike, and plugged them both in, but the needle on the audio gauge didn't move.

"Oh, no," Erin moaned. "These mikes aren't working."

"Don't panic. They're not turned on yet," Matt informed her.

"Whew, *that* was a close one. I thought I'd have to eat my words."

Matt put a reassuring hand on her shoulder. "Just relax and concentrate on what you're doing. If you think about all the possible things that might go wrong, they will. I guarantee it."

One by one they turned each piece of equipment on and got ready to interview the two girls at the first table who were folding squares of colored paper into intricate figures: a frog, a crane, a flower, a cricket, and more. Erin held her breath until the tape began to roll. They had agreed that Matt would work the camera and she would ask questions for the first few interviews. Then they would switch.

Next they moved down to the end of the table where another girl, dressed in a beautiful silk kimono, was demonstrating flower arranging.

As they worked their way down the aisle of booths, they stopped to watch some Israeli students filling pita bread with Middle Eastern salad.

"Let's stop for a snack," Erin suggested when the aroma reminded her that she had skipped dinner.

"We're on duty now. Work before play, you know," Matt said in a mock-professional voice.

"Could we at least beg a free sample?" she pleaded, eyeing a booth for egg rolls up ahead.

"Nope, we've got to finish these booths before the crowds get too heavy and start pushing in front of the camera."

"Slave driver," she muttered.

"Plotting a rebellion?"

"Only if it means that you'll carry all the equipment," she replied.

"No such luck. Speaking of which—"

"I know, I know. It's my turn for the camera, isn't it?"

Their bantering had put her at ease. Cautiously, Erin picked up the camera, still attached to the tripod, and carried it over to the next exhibit, Ukranian egg decorating. Two girls in colorful aprons over wide skirts sat painting intricate traditional designs onto hollowed out egg shells. Erin looked back over her shoulder at the monitor to see if the color was okay. Not too bad, she thought.

"Maybe we should pull back these lights a little," she said to Matt. "Her face looks sort of washed out, don't you think?"

"You're right," he agreed as he put down the microphone and began to drag one of the light stands farther away from the subject.

Erin was glad that he'd agreed with her judgment and now began to handle the camera with genuine confidence. She avoided the bright white of their blouses and zoomed in on the delicate detail of the design.

By this time the gym had become crowded, and it was getting difficult to move. People kept stopping in front of the camera and tripping over the wires.

"Let's leave the booths and get some of the concert in the auditorium," Matt said.

After some complicated juggling of equipment they made their way to the auditorium where they caught the end of the Russian folk songs and stayed on to get a Greek line dance with the members of the audience coming up onstage to join the dancers.

After about an hour of music and dancing, Matt said with a yawn, "Let's call it a night."

"I was hoping you'd say that soon," Erin replied gratefully. "My shoulder is about to break in two."

"Why didn't you say so? I could have taken over. I thought you *wanted* to do it," Matt kidded.

"I did want to. It's just that now I want to quit. I suddenly realized I'm starving to death, and I can't hold this thing for one more minute."

Awkwardly Erin swung the camera down from her shoulder, cradling it in both arms as she tried to move her cramped muscles.

"Here, let me rub that shoulder for a minute," Matt said.

He reached over and placed his hand on her slender shoulder, pressing his thumb into the sore muscle.

"Oooh, that feels good," she said softly. "Keep it up. A little more to the left. Now to the right and down a little. That's better. Mmmm . . ."

"You'll have to get some muscle on those little bones of yours if you expect to do much video. Even the Minicams get heavy after a while," he said. "Is the camera turned off?"

"It is now," Erin answered as she flipped the switch.

"Okay, let's see how fast we can break down and get this stuff out of here. We'll go for a record."

"You bet."

Twenty minutes was the best they could do, but finally the equipment was safely stowed in the trunk of Matt's car. They returned to the gym for their well-deserved snack to find it practically deserted, the food booths already closed. Almost everyone was in the auditorium watching the show, and the few people left in the gym were packing up their equipment and sweeping up the trash.

"Looks like we're out of luck here," Matt said. "I guess it'll have to be pizza for us now. How about Regina's?"

"Sounds good to me," Erin agreed.

Instead of sitting across from her as he had at the ice-cream parlor, Matt slid into the booth at the pizza parlor beside her. He casually draped his arm around her shoulders as they studied the large red menu in the dim light. As Erin leaned her head against his shoulder and gazed at the stubby candle flickering in a bowl on their table, she realized how exhausted she was—physically and emotionally.

"Order anything that's quick," she said. "I'm fading fast. If I don't get something to eat soon, you may have to carry me home."

"Well, I wouldn't mind that," Matt said, brushing his tanned cheek against her silky blond hair.

While Matt ordered a mushroom pizza, Erin closed her eyes and let herself enjoy the luxurious feeling of his arm around her.

"You're not falling asleep on me, are you?" Matt whispered.

"No, I'm just trying to relax," she said, looking up with a smile. "Hey, I just remembered, my mom put an apple in my bag. Want a piece?"

"Sure, let me cut it for you."

Erin reached into her bag and brought out the apple, and Matt quartered it with his Swiss army knife which he produced from one of the many zippered pockets in his jacket.

"Here, have an hors d'oeuvre," he said, nodding slightly.

"Why, thank you. That looks delicious," she answered in her best English accent.

They ate the apple slowly and then devoured the hot pizza the waitress set before them.

Matt finished the last three pieces while Erin sipped the last of her soda.

"I thought you said you were starving," Matt said skeptically. "You only ate two pieces."

"I was starving. But even when I'm starving I never eat more than two pieces. Besides, that apple took the edge off my appetite."

"You mean half an apple," he said with a

smile. "I'm not complaining, though. By the time the pizza came I was starving, too. Anyway I love to take out girls who can't finish their dinners."

Erin looked up. "Really?"

"Yeah. I have a big appetite, and one and a half orders is just about right for me," he said, laughing.

"Well, then I'm your girl," Erin said, blushing as she realized how obvious that sounded.

"I *hope* you will be," Matt said gently. "You know you're really something special, Erin. You're so different from the Preston Academy girls. They're so used to having their own way all the time that they all act like princesses."

Erin couldn't believe her ears. She never thought she'd compare favorably to the sophisticated and talented private school girls.

"Actually one girl in my painting class *is* a princess," he went on. "Her father is an Arabian sheikh. And she's the only girl in the class who *isn't* stuck up."

"Oh, Matt," Erin said.

"Working with you has been fun," he said seriously.

"It's been fun for me, too," she said.

About ten people were standing at the front

of the restaurant waiting for seats, and the waitress impatiently asked them for the second time if they wanted to order anything else.

"I think it's time to move on," Matt said reluctantly.

Not again, Erin thought. Every time they really started talking, something was sure to break it up. "Matt, would you do me a favor?" she asked as she slipped on her jacket.

"Sure, anything," he agreed without hesitation.

"Would you walk me home? It's less than a mile."

"I'll do better than that. I'll drive you home. I'm a guy with wheels, remember?"

"I know. But it's such a beautiful night. Just leave your car in the parking lot, and you can walk back and get it later."

He looked at her for a moment as if she had lost her mind and then shook his head, grinning. "Well, I guess the equipment will be all right in the trunk. Come on, let's go."

They headed down the tree-lined street, arms entwined. It felt like fall—not too cold, but crisp and clear. Erin thought she had never seen so many stars in the city sky.

"So you like walking," Matt said.

"Yeah, on nights like this. I—I just wanted a chance to talk. It's hard having a really good conversation with someone while they're driving. They never really pay attention to what you're saying."

He drew her close to his side. "You're probably right. You know I haven't walked anywhere since my mom gave me her old car when I turned sixteen. I may be missing something."

"It's supposed to be very healthy for you," Erin said.

"And cheap, too. Would you be interested in going on a walk date?" he asked with a grin.

"I might be. Where did you want to walk to?"

"Well, this weekend let's walk downtown to Quincy Market, get some lunch, and eat it in the waterfront park," he began. "Then next weekend we can do the river walk—"

"Wait a minute," Erin said, laughing. "Let's go back to Quincy Market. Do you know how far that is?"

"Oh, maybe three or four miles."

"When I said I liked to walk I meant three or four blocks, not miles," she said with a groan. "But I guess I'll give it a try."

"I knew you were brave," he told her. "Don't worry, we can always take public transportation home if we get too worn out."

They continued on, arm in arm, talking about friends and school and even whether or not there were extraterrestrials. Matt was convinced there were. Erin wasn't so sure. She only knew that she had never been with a boy who was so easy to talk to. Before she knew it, they were standing in front of her house. They fell silent as they realized the evening was coming to an end.

"You were right," Matt said at last. "That *was* nice. I just wish I didn't have to turn around and walk back to the car by myself, now."

"Well, I'll walk back with you then," Erin offered with a grin.

They turned around and walked all the way back to the restaurant, discussing their plans for the weekend.

"Okay," Matt said as his car came into sight. "This time I *am* going to drive you home. Otherwise we'll be going back and forth all night, and I have a lab report to write up."

Erin laughed. She liked the thought of walking with him all night long.

They hopped into the car and were back at Erin's house in less than ten minutes.

"There you are!" her mother exclaimed as the car pulled into the drive. Obviously, she'd been waiting by the front window. "Where in the world have you been? I thought I saw you in the driveway a half hour ago, and then you suddenly disappeared."

"We were getting worried, Erin," her father said, joining in. "The festival has been over for two hours, young lady."

"I'm sorry, Mr. Marksson," Matt said quickly, explaining why it had taken so long to get home.

"Well, I'd rather you both save these walks of yours for the daytime from now on," her father said.

"That's exactly what we're going to do, Dad," Erin promised as she waved goodbye to Matt and went up the front walk with her parents.

Chapter Ten

Erin was in a fantastic mood all the next day, Friday. The whole world looked wonderful to her. She hardly noticed when Davy burned her toast at breakfast; she didn't get angry when Leslie spilled milk on her shoe at lunch; and she just smiled when Mr. Crabtree insisted that she copy her entire lab report over in pen. She was happily floating, oblivious of the world passing by, just waiting for the end of school when she could see Matt again at video class.

Two-thirty, free at last, she thought as she pushed open one of the heavy double doors of the high school and set off across the lawn.

Leslie had to stay after to make up a quiz she had missed, but Erin was eager to get to the studio. She went on ahead, glancing behind her from time to time hoping to catch a glimpse of Matt's Saab.

She walked quickly for the first two blocks so she'd be ahead of the kids beginning to stream out of school. Then she slowed down as her thoughts turned to Matt.

It was funny, she thought, how a person could spend years going out with boys without ever finding anyone special, then—wham! suddenly love would strike. Matt seemed so different from most of the boys she knew. She had to admit that his going to a fancy private school made him seem a little exotic and more mature.

She couldn't possibly feel romantic about someone like Jeff, whom she'd been neighbors with for ages and who used to pull her braids in kindergarten and tried to wash her face in the snow as recently as the sixth grade. Leslie probably liked him because she had only moved to Ashboro two years before when he had already outgrown his most obnoxious stages, Erin decided. She wondered if Matt had ever been obnoxious. She'd have to ask his sister about that.

She had gone another block before she heard the now-familiar sound of his car coming up behind her.

"Where's the gang?" he asked as he leaned over the front seat to push open the door on her side.

"Oh, Leslie had to stay after school. They'll be along in a while."

"Should we wait?"

"She's taking a quiz, and Jeff is waiting for her. I'm not sure how long they'll be. I think we'd better go or we'll miss the beginning of class. What are we doing today, anyway?"

"Advanced logging and editing, according to the schedule," Matt answered as he pulled back into traffic.

"Advanced editing?"

"We'll need it for our festival piece. It's stuff like how to keep the audio track with the interview questions on the tape while inserting new video shots over it to cover mistakes. That can be tricky."

They parked and went upstairs, and found, to their surprise, that the studio door was locked.

"Let's find out what's going on," Matt said, glancing at his watch.

They walked back to the reception area

where the secretary told them that Eve hadn't arrived yet. "She just called a few minutes ago to say she got held up at a meeting and asked me to tell you all to wait. She'll be about twenty minutes."

Matt turned to Erin. "Want to take a walk down by the river till everyone gets here?" he asked.

"Sure," she answered.

They crossed the main boulevard and followed the sidewalk along the upper level till they reached some stairs that led down to the grassy area at the foot of the bridge.

Erin, glad for the chance to be alone with Matt, was surprised to find that her thoughts kept wandering to the video. "You know this class is really important to me," she confessed as they began to walk along the bank. "I really want to do a good job."

"Me, too. I can't stand it when I screw up. Eve said I had a good chance of winning an award this year. I entered my tape last year, but the competition was pretty stiff."

"I wish people thought I was very good at something," Erin said. "It's sort of depressing when all your friends are really talented people, and you've got nothing special. Like, Jeff has been ice-skating since he was three and will probably be captain of the hockey team. And Leslie gives special piano recitals and has gotten tons of awards. She even played at Symphony Hall once."

"Did you ever take lessons or anything?" Matt inquired.

"I did, but I guess my parents were pretty easygoing about it. They always said 'Do what you want.' So I never stuck with anything more than a few months. Sometimes I wish they had forced me to become a ballerina or something."

"You?" he asked with considerable amusement.

"Well, maybe not a ballerina. It wouldn't have worked, anyway. Imagine taking all those years of lessons and then getting passed over for being too short."

"That happened to me, sort of," Matt confided. "For a while I wanted to be a jockey. I took tons of riding lessons and helped out at my uncle's pony farm a couple of summers. Then I started growing. And grew, and grew— But I still have fun riding."

"I guess I've never taken anything really seriously before," Erin admitted reluctantly.

"When you find something you really love and are willing to work hard and give up some things to do it, you'll be good at it," Matt said. "I *know* you will."

"How did you get involved in video?" she asked.

"My dad works at Channel Five, and he used to take me with him to work sometimes. I was fascinated by the lights and cameras. I used to sit in the back of the studio while he was in meetings and dream about when I would be big enough to work a camera. Sometimes they'd let me go into the control room and push a few buttons. I'd go wild when they let me wear the headphones. At home I'd play director for weeks after that. So this is pretty much a dream come true for me. I could do it night and day, no trouble."

"Me, too. I hope the stuff we shot last night is good. It's just got to be," Erin said.

"Don't bet on it. You've got to be prepared for a few setbacks. Once I accidentally erased something I'd spent ten hours taping. I was so disgusted I couldn't even *watch* TV for a week afterward without getting upset. If you're serious about video, you'll probably have a lot of 'learning experiences' like that."

"I hope not," Erin murmured. "I don't think I could take it."

They climbed up on a flat rock that jutted

out from the bank of the Charles River, and Erin pulled her sweater more tightly around her as the river breezes whipped her hair back from her face.

Matt put his arm around her to shield her from the wind, and she felt the rough wool of his fisherman's knit sweater brush against her cheek. She nestled cozily against his chest. Together they gazed across the quiet river to the yacht club on the other bank. The sound of the chugging motor of a huge cabin cruiser carried across the water as it moved away from the far dock and maneuvered out to sea. They watched until the luxurious vessel was only a white speck on the horizon.

Erin loved feeling Matt's strong arms around her and the gentle movement of his chest against her back as he breathed. They sat silently for a while, enjoying the watery smell in the air and following the sailboats tacking back and forth in the stiff breeze.

Matt leaned over and touched his lips to her hair, sending a shiver of delight all the way down to her toes. Erin turned slightly, looking up at him as he bent lower and gently kissed her forehead, brushing back the blond wisps that fluttered around her delicate face. She arched her neck, stretching up toward him, and their lips met at last, clinging together for a few delicious seconds as Erin slipped her arm around his waist and held him close.

She was a little surprised at herself—at the vigor of her response. But she had been waiting for that moment for ages it seemed, and when it happened she simply went with it, letting herself feel the pure thrill of being with him. She had always been a little shy about expressing her interest in a boy, but now that Matt had taken the initiative, her shyness vanished. As she settled back in his arms, she only wished he'd do it again.

"Hey," he said, glancing at his watch. "Let's get going. It's two forty-five. Everyone must be there by now."

He took her hand, pulling her up the embankment. They crossed the street and ran the few blocks back to the studio, claiming the last two seats in the room. Erin's heart was beating furiously, and her face was flushed—partly from the run and partly from the exhilaration of that first kiss.

"We were just about to start without you," Eve said as she handed them the last two sets of mimeographed notes. "Some delays

130

are inevitable," she added, looking down at them over the tops of her glasses. "But lateness on the part of crew members is unacceptable."

Erin, still in a happy daze, was brought back to reality by the brusqueness in Eve's reprimand.

Eve began the class with a review of basic editing from the week before. Then they viewed a tape compiled by Eve that contained every possible editing mistake, from jump cuts, where joining two dissimilar views make the subject seem to jump to a new position, to the worst possible mistake, loss of control track, where blank tape flashes between edits.

"To avoid these errors," Eve began after the break, "you need precise logging and a good editing script. I'd like to look at somebody's raw footage now, so we can talk about some actual editing decisions. Any volunteers?"

Matt raised his hand.

"Matt and Erin? Good. Go get your tape out of the cabinet and give it to the technician," she said. "First we'll just eyeball it to see what we're dealing with here."

"Why'd you let her show ours?" Erin whispered to Matt as he sat down again.

"I wanted her opinion. She's a tough critic, but she knows her stuff," he replied.

The tape began to roll on the monitor. Erin cringed as she noticed every shake of the camera, every streak of trailing white from a window or ceiling light caught in the field of vision, every blurry image and awkward hesitation in the dialogue.

Erin glanced over at Eve who was jotting down notes on a pad of yellow paper. Then she looked at Matt. He was studying the tape intently but didn't look too upset.

"It's awful," she whispered.

"Nah, it's not too bad," he reassured her. "There are plenty of decent parts. That's what editing's for. It doesn't matter how much bad stuff you've got as long as there are a few good shots for the final version."

Erin was not totally convinced.

When they reached the end of the last act that she had taped, instead of switching to the snowy pattern of a blank tape, the footage kept rolling. The camera had dipped to a crazy angle so the lens was pointing up at the far corner of the ceiling, directly into the lights. The image hung there jiggling occasionally, leaving bright light trails tinged with green flickering across the screen.

The next minute lasted an eternity. When would it end? She heard Matt swearing under his breath. Eve was drumming her pencil against her clipboard, and her mouth was drawn into a tense line. Erin was about to have a "learning experience," and it didn't look as though it would be a very pleasant one.

"Class, please take out your list of rules for using the camera. Miss Marksson," Eve said harshly, "could you read rule number one, please."

"Never point a video camera directly at a source of light," Erin read inaudibly.

"That is correct. Do you know why this is the first rule in the book, Miss Marksson?"

Erin shook her head, not trusting her voice.

"Exposure to light like this can burn out the vidicon tube of a camera, that's why. You can do thousands of dollars worth of damage to the equipment.

"Mr. Blakeslee," she went on, her face reddening with anger, "could you please read rule number two."

"Always turn off the camera and replace the lens cap as soon as you are finished shooting. Never leave the camera running unless you are looking through the viewfinder."

"Are those instructions clear to you, Mr. Blakeslee?"

"Yes, ma'am," Matt answered quietly.

"Do you have any excuse for this serious lapse in video procedures?" she asked, sounding like the captain of a ship speaking to a mutinous crew.

"No," he said flatly. "I guess we just forgot to turn the camera off right way. I'm sorry."

Erin felt like sinking through the floor. It wasn't *we*. It was *she* who had forgotten. She had been so interested in getting that back rub that she hadn't thought about the camera at all. And now Matt was taking the blame for her.

"It's not Matt's fault, Eve. I was holding the camera. I guess I just wasn't thinking," Erin admitted.

"Nevertheless, I do hold you *both* personally responsible for any damage that may have been done to that camera. Matt, you are the more experienced member of your team, and it's your responsibility to help our newer interns learn how to handle the equipment properly."

Now Matt's face was beginning to show red through his fading summer tan. The big shot of the class had made one of the stupidest mistakes possible, according to Eve.

Eve turned to the class. "We're professionals here, and I expect professional behavior from all of you. In my days at the networks, people were fired, on the spot, for less," she added tersely.

Matt has made a stupid mistake, thought Erin. But it wasn't pointing the camera at a light for a few minutes. It was falling for her and choosing her for a video partner. She was wrecking his chance for success at the thing he'd dreamed about since childhood.

Suddenly Erin jumped up and ran from the room. She couldn't stand to see Matt humiliated in front of all the interns because of her. She was a jinx.

She ran from the studio and down the embankment to the river and walked along it for about a mile, barely noticing the tears falling from her eyes.

Chapter Eleven

It was well over an hour later that Erin finally made her way home and slipped up to her room. She had walked most of the way down to the sailboat dock before turning back, and now her feet ached. She kicked off her shoes and buried her head in her pillow, not wanting to talk to anyone.

"Erin, you're *here*!" her mother exclaimed when she finally came downstairs. "I didn't see you come in. Matt has called three times and Leslie, twice. I'm afraid I told them both you weren't home yet."

"That's okay, Mom. I don't feel like talking

to anyone right now. I'll call them back after dinner."

"What's the matter, dear? You look as if you just lost your best friend."

Tears began to well up in Erin's eyes again, and she didn't trust herself to speak without breaking down and crying.

Instead, she sat down at the kitchen table and covered her face with her hands, trying to regain her composure.

"Want to tell me what happened?" her mother said softly.

"I made a mistake on our shoot last night," Erin began as she reached for a napkin to dab her eyes. "I recorded a few minutes of ceiling lights at the end of the tape, and Matt got in trouble for it."

"Did you explain that it was your fault?" Mrs. Marksson asked.

"Sure, but Eve said Matt was responsible, anyway, because he's had more experience."

"Was he angry with you?"

"I don't know—I left. He should have been. I'm really messing things up for him."

"We all make mistakes. It's part of learning," her mother told her.

"But Eve always gave him a lot of responsibility, and now he's let her down by teaming up with me," Erin sobbed.

"Well, why don't you call him back," her mother said reasonably. "Maybe he's not as upset about this as you are."

"But that's not the point, Mom. Nobody wants to have one of the Three Stooges for a video partner."

"It still wouldn't hurt to talk about it, and I *did* promise I'd have you call him back as soon as you got in. He sounded very anxious to talk to you."

Erin shrugged.

She sat silently through dinner, eating little and not responding to her brother's attempts to joke around. When the phone rang, she didn't even look up as Davy raced into the hall to get it.

"For you, Erin," he called back.

She got up slowly and went to answer it. It was Matt.

"Erin, I've been trying to get you all afternoon. How come you split?"

She took a deep breath, willing herself not to start crying again. "I couldn't take it. It wasn't fair for Eve to blame you for my mistake. I thought I'd better get out of there before I said something that would get us into more trouble."

"Yeah, I was furious, too, at first. At both of us."

"But it was *my* fault," Erin argued.

"No, I should've known better."

"Well, she didn't have to be so mean in front of the whole class."

"If she didn't get mad, people would get sloppy. Anyway, I wanted to tell you, we checked out the camera after class, and it doesn't seem to be damaged. We were lucky. It was jiggling around so much while I was rubbing your back that no one spot got burned."

Erin's heart slowed down a little. "That's a relief. I was wondering what my dad would say when he had to pay the three-hundred-dollar deductible on the studio insurance. I don't even have that much in my savings account."

"Well, we're off the hook this time, but no more—"

"I know, I know," Erin said. "Matt, I think it would be better if I didn't work as your partner anymore."

"I didn't mean . . ." Matt said, sounding

upset. "I just meant we'd have to be more careful, that's all."

"But I'm trying as hard as I can," she said, her voice shaking. "I just can't remember everything one hundred percent. And it makes me more nervous when I know that I'm ruining things for you, too."

"You're not ruining things. You're making it a lot more fun for me."

"I know that on your own you would do a terrific project. You're sure to win an award at the state video convention. I don't want to hold you back from doing your best work."

"Erin, I make mistakes, too, you know. You just haven't caught me in any big ones yet. That's why it's good to be a team. One person remembers what the other one forgets."

Erin was not convinced. "So far, you've done all the remembering, and I've done all the forgetting, and that makes me feel pretty dumb."

"Well, you've had some good ideas, and that's important. And it's fun just to be with you." He paused. "And you helped carry the equipment," he added lamely, trying to think of anything that might make her feel useful.

But it had just the opposite effect.

"Matt, you're just trying to make me feel

better. You know I'm not strong enough to carry the heavy things, and I don't want to be just a girl companion. If I can't be a real partner, I'd rather struggle along on my own and know that whatever work I did was mine, good or bad," she said vehemently.

Sensing that the conversation was taking a wrong turn, Matt changed the subject.

"Let's sleep on it, okay? Don't forget we have a date at the waterfront tomorrow. I'll stop by for you around ten."

"Oh, I don't know if I'll feel like—"

"Don't try to get out of it," Matt interrupted. "We have a definite date, and I expect you to keep it. I've already made reservations for two for a spot along the dock," he said, joking. "See you tomorrow."

Erin was too upset to start another argument, but now she really wasn't looking forward to that long walk with Matt. All she wanted to do was hide.

Five minutes after she finished talking with Matt, the phone rang again. It was Leslie.

"I'll take this one upstairs," she called to Davy.

She went up to her room and settled into the pillows in the corner, then picked up the phone.

"Erin, where did you run off to?" Leslie asked as soon as she heard Erin's voice.

"Oh, I walked down by the river to cool off. I couldn't take it anymore."

"Old Eve *was* pretty hard on you guys. She acts like we're working for a big production company instead of doing student projects," Leslie complained.

"I guess I don't blame her," Erin said. "She's just trying to teach us what it's like in the real world."

"How did Matt take it?"

"I'm going to work on my own from now on," Erin said determinedly.

"What?" Leslie asked indignantly. "You mean he's so mad he doesn't want to be your partner anymore? That toad! Anybody could've made a mistake like that. How could he dump you after all the work you've put in?"

"No, it's not Matt. He wanted to keep working together. It's me. I don't want to hold him back. I'd feel terrible if he didn't get a good grade or didn't win an award because of me. Just the idea of it is making me nervous, and I'm bound to goof up again."

"Hmmm, I see what you mean," her friend agreed. "But it'll be hard working alone. You know, the equipment and everything."

"Say, Leslie, since you and Jeff haven't done very much on your second project, do you think you could switch and be my partner?" Erin asked.

"But Jeff and I are doing okay now. We're starting to get something accomplished. It's actually turning out to be fun. Otherwise I'd be happy to switch."

"What did you decide to do?"

"We're going to interview my grandmother and Jeff's great-uncle about what it was like when their families first came to the States and how they felt about the Statue of Liberty."

"That sounds good."

"I'm keeping my fingers crossed. Tomorrow's our big day. I'm going to be the boss for the segment about Grandma D'Amico, and Jeff'll be in charge of the other part—. But what about you, Erin? What are you going to do? You're right in the middle of your multicultural project."

"Oh, I don't know, Leslie. What should I do? I'm so miserable. Maybe I should change my mind. But even if Matt isn't mad this time, he's bound to get annoyed eventually. I couldn't stand to have him mad at me, but I don't want him to overlook my mistakes or take the blame for me, either."

"You could keep trying and see what happens," Leslie advised optimistically.

"Things might just get worse."

"Or better," Leslie suggested.

"This video course was my big chance. I wanted to prove I could be really good at something. Instead, I'm proving that I'm a klutz," Erin said hopelessly.

"This does sound serious," Leslie admitted sympathetically. "But my philosophy is still 'wait and see.' Things can always take a turn for the better."

"Well, we still have a date for tomorrow morning. I didn't even want to keep that after today. But Matt insisted."

"Then just go and try to have fun. I think you're taking this whole thing too seriously."

"You're too sensible," Erin muttered. "But I'll try. I'll call you tomorrow night."

"Hope everything works out. 'Bye."

Erin decided to go to bed and not think about anything until after she had seen Matt again. Then maybe she could sort out her feelings better.

At ten o'clock sharp the next morning, Matt pulled up in front of her house looking very cool in his baggy pants with the extra pockets and a gray windbreaker. Erin was glad she had gotten up early to take some extra time to shower and dress. She had even ironed her shirt, which was sort of a once-a-year event in the Marksson household. She tied her pale blue sweater, the one that perfectly matched her eyes, loosely around her shoulders, picked up her bag, and they were off.

As they approached Boston's business section they turned down Beacon Street, following the trolley tracks toward the city. They strolled past the Saturday shoppers and bumper-to-bumper traffic and entered a neighborhood of old, elegant apartment buildings.

In the distance they could see the modern, blue-green facade of the Hancock Building reflecting bright sky and cloud shadows on its glass surface. They picked up their pace as they passed through a university neighborhood. Everyone seemed to be in a rush there, hurrying to class, getting fast food in the student hangouts that lined the street, pushing to board the overcrowded trolleys.

Erin didn't want to talk about the video class, but she was at a loss for words. Even Matt, who could always keep a conversation lively, was unusually quiet.

When they finally arrived downtown at the

edge of the Public Gardens, Matt declared it was time for a break. He bought them each a gigantic hot pretzel from a sidewalk vendor, and they entered the park to find a free bench. Although it was October, a few of the summer flowers—the petunias and the marigolds—were still in bloom. But the beds of mums in their fall rusty tones and the brilliantly turning leaves of the maple trees dominated the scene.

"You know, I almost never come down here," Erin said. "I don't know why. It's so pretty. I just never think of it. How about you?"

"I used to come down pretty often. My mom used to bring my sister and me down to art fairs and music festivals on the Common. They were fun. There'd always be face painting and magicians or jugglers, music, things like that."

"Oh, we went to a few of those. Davy was so cute, the magicians always chose him to come up and pick a card. He's been doing card tricks ever since."

Matt laughed. "What I liked best, though, were the mounted policemen. I was terrified when one rode by. I'd be staring right at the guy's big, black boot. But I loved to watch them from a distance. It drove my mom nuts.

There she was, exposing me to all these cultural activities in the city, and I couldn't take my eyes off the cop on his big horse."

After a brief rest they continued strolling, crossing over the pond where the swan boats filled with tourists paddled along, then stopping where a crowd had gathered to listen to a street musician.

When the guitarist stopped for a break, Erin and Matt moved on, crossing the street and entering the Common. There was more open space there. Cows had grazed on the Common in colonial times, and the hilly, curving paths provided a challenge for skateboarders who had taken over an area near the fountains to practice their tricks.

"I came down here when I was shooting my skateboarding tape," Matt said. "There's always someone here showing off. I had a lot of trouble with people walking in front of my camera right in the middle of something good, though. You'd think they could wait a minute. And the little kids kept running up and putting their faces right next to the lens and waving. I sure had a lot of junk on that tape."

Erin's mood began to change. She had been enjoying herself till then. Just walking beside Matt, trying to match his long, easy gait made her feel happy. She had tried to put the day before out of her mind as if it had never happened. But as he began to talk about video, she felt her stomach begin to churn.

Matt noticed the change at once. "What's the matter, Erin? I guess I must be boring you with this play-by-play account of my project."

"No, it's not that—" she said.

"What is it, then?" he asked, genuinely puzzled.

"It's just that, the more you talk about video, the more I realize how important it is to you. And how serious you are about doing it well. I may never live up to your standards."

"Maybe not," he retorted, grinning. "But I don't either."

"Don't what?"

"Live up to my standards. That's what I've been telling you these past fifteen minutes. All the stupid things I did."

"Well, that's different."

"No, it isn't."

"Yes, it is," she said. "Because *your* tape turned out wonderfully in the end."

"Well, *our* tape will turn out well, too, if you'll just relax and give it a chance."

"I don't think I can," Erin said, afraid that

she was going to start crying. "I'm so nervous about making a mistake; I feel so awkward and clumsy. I'm bound to create another catastrophe sooner or later, and I'd never forgive myself if I messed things up for you, too. I think I'll be better off working on my own or with someone at my own level. And so would you."

Matt continued to try to talk her out of it.

"Come on, we're right in the middle of something, and I need your help," he said, arguing with her.

"You don't, really," she answered.

For the first time she saw real anger in his eyes. "You know," he said, "I'm starting to feel pretty foolish. I thought you liked me. Maybe it was my imagination."

"I *do* like you, Matt. I-I've never liked anyone so much."

"Well, then, I don't understand why you want to quit."

"I just told you," Erin said, more to herself than to him.

They had emerged from the Common now and were heading toward the historic district, the skyscrapers and the gold dome of the State House behind them.

"How about weekends?" Matt asked, starting to look miserable.

"I don't know," Erin answered softly. "I don't feel very good about myself right now, and I need some time to work things out."

They arrived at Quincy Market, bought two portions of fried clams from a seafood cart, and carried them down to the dock to eat. A gray-flecked sea gull circled them, then perched on a nearby post waiting for scraps. Dark clouds rolled in from the ocean, covering the sun and making the chilly sea breeze even colder.

"I can't believe you're going to be so stubborn about this," Matt said.

"I have to do what I think is best," Erin replied, pulling her sweater more tightly around her.

For a moment Matt looked as if he was going to argue further. Then Erin saw his eyes become distant. "Let's go," he said abruptly.

The squawking sea gull protested as they got up and threw away their leftovers in the covered trash barrel. They boarded a trolley and barely exchanged another word during the half-hour ride home.

"What about the festival footage?" Matt

asked, trying one more time as he got into his car, which he'd left in front of her house.

"You finish that one if you want. I'd rather start over."

"I don't believe you," he said, sounding shaken.

Erin felt terrible. She was hurting him, and she knew it. "I'm not going to change my mind," she said gently. "It'll be better if you finish it yourself."

"Then we might as well erase it, because I'd rather start over, too," he said angrily.

"Whatever you say," she mumbled, wishing desperately that things weren't turning out that way.

Matt looked furious. "I don't have anything else to say to you!"

Erin shut her eyes against her tears as Matt got into his car, slammed the door, and roared off. How could making the right decision hurt so much? She knew that she needed to prove something to herself, even if it meant giving up love—for a while.

Chapter Twelve

The next day was the worst of her life. Erin missed Matt terribly. Every time the phone rang, in the split second before the caller said hello, she would think it was he. She must have picked up the phone a hundred times, starting to call him, just to hear his voice. Only her pride stopped her from going through with it.

She kept replaying their final awful fight in her mind. There was a good chance she had lost his friendship as well as his love, and she couldn't bear the thought of that. If only she could make him understand. It wasn't that she had to be as good as he was, she just wanted to be in the same ballpark. If two people wanted to work together on the same thing, they had to respect each other. One couldn't be winning prizes while the other fell on his or, in this case, her face.

As she did her Sunday chores she forced herself to keep Matt in the back of her mind and focus on the task she had set herself. First of all, she'd have to come up with a new idea. Ideas, she was good at—carrying them out was the tough part. Her main problem would be the equipment. She could barely lug around half of it, so taking everything herself would be impossible. For a wild minute she considered asking Davy to come with her and carry the light stuff. *Forget it,* she told herself, envisioning the shelves of broken toys that lined his room. It was just possible that klutziness ran in their family.

She took a basketful of clean clothes from the dryer and brought them into her room. She began to fold them, thinking of posssible solutions to her problem. *I'll have to switch from three-quarter inch to half-inch tape,* she thought as she matched socks and rolled each pair together. That equipment was much smaller and easier for one person to handle. And if she chose a subject that could be taped outdoors, she could eliminate the lights, the adapter, the monitor, and all the extension cords, leaving only batteries to think about. That would make everything *much* more manageable.

Erin smiled hopefully. Maybe she *could* come up with the answers, she thought, if she could just do it her own way at her own speed. She took the empty basket back down to the laundry room and switched another load of wash to the dryer. There was only one thing she regretted. She didn't look forward to Monday at the studio the way she had been. In fact, she dreaded it. Sitting by herself while everyone else was teamed up with a partner would be pretty depressing. She'd have to take even more careful notes than before since she couldn't count on anyone but herself to get the information.

Monday's video class was almost as bad as she had expected. She sat by herself, feeling empty without Matt beside her. Both of them were going out of their way to avoid the other, though Matt didn't have to work too hard at it. He was easily the most popular guy in the class, and there always seemed to be someone beside him, asking for advice. Erin felt a twinge of jealousy. She missed that advice. She missed his gentle teasing and kidding around. She missed everything about Matt Blakeslee.

She stared down at the piece of paper on her desk and determinedly added another idea to the list of things she could film on her own. "Roller-skating," she wrote, then crossed it out as she realized the idea had come indirectly from Matt's skateboarding film. Reflexively, she looked around the room for him. He was nowhere in sight, but she noticed that Jeff and Leslie were at it again. Leslie was sitting with her arms folded defiantly while Jeff was standing over her, looking as though he were ready to put his fist through the wall. Erin couldn't make out what he was saying from across the room, but it didn't look complimentary.

Erin went back to her list and considered the ideas one by one. Number seventeen was pumpkins. That might be it. Everybody was interested in pumpkins around Halloween. It would be colorful, and she could shoot it outside. She could imagine the opening scene, hundreds of pumpkins piled up at a roadside stand. Then she would cut to people carving them, followed by scenes of neighborhood porches on Halloween night. Excitedly, Erin started to make notes.

Leslie flopped down in the empty chair beside her. "If that offer of yours is still good, I want to take you up on it now. Jeff is being totally impossible. He's really driving me up the wall this time," she said angrily.

"Well, we could try it," Erin said doubtfully, having just gotten used to the idea of working solo. "I guess two heads *are* better than one."

"Here's my new list of ideas. What do you think of this one?" she asked, going on to explain the pumpkin idea to Leslie, who seemed agreeable to anything that didn't include Jeff.

"There's just one thing you have to promise, though," Erin finished. "You can't change your mind and go back with Jeff in the middle of this project. Knowing you two, you're bound to kiss and make up sooner or later."

Leslie sighed. "I hope so, but I promise I'll stick with you for the video no matter what he says."

"Then it's a deal."

"But the same goes for you. Don't you dare get lovesick and go back as Matt's partner, either."

Erin hesitated a moment, wondering if Matt could persuade her to abandon her friend. Then she promised. They okayed the switch with Eve and reserved the camera for later in the week. That day it was Jeff who left early and walked home by himself.

On Friday Mrs. Marksson let Erin drive the car out to one of the roadside stands where piles of freshly picked pumpkins lined the stubbly fields. Erin and Leslie had picked a beautiful Indian summer day, and the taping went as smoothly as could be expected for two novices.

"Let's drive over to my house and take a look at the tape right away on my VCR," Leslie suggested as they drove back into town.

They raced into the living room and slipped their tape into the machine. The color was strange for the first five minutes. They had forgotten to put the outdoor filter on the lens. After that had been remedied, the oranges were more orange and the greens more green. But the rest of the tape looked as though it had been made from a roller-coaster ride. The camera didn't stay on anything more than a few seconds. Even then it jiggled and went in and out of focus. They had made all the classic mistakes of beginners. Not being content to find a shot and stick with it, they had zoomed in and zoomed out, panned back and forth, followed people around with jerky, bobbing movements, and generally made a quiet vegetable stand look like a three-ring circus.

Erin was devastated.

"We're going to do this over again," she said. "Tomorrow."

"It's not that bad, is it?" asked Leslie, whose standards were a little lower. "I think I saw a few good shots in the beginning that we could use."

"That was before we put the filter on," Erin reminded her. "No, I see what we have to do now. We've got to tape it again. And next time we'll wait for a few good shots and hold them longer. We can't keep changing our minds and moving the camera all over the place."

"All right," Leslie said, resigned to spending another afternoon in the country. "This means I'm going to be up half the night practicing for my recital, you know. I hope we start learning fast, because I don't have time to do everything twice."

"That's all right. If this one doesn't come out better, I'll do it again myself," Erin said. "I'm going to make a good tape if it kills me."

They returned to the stand the next day, to the surprise of the owner who couldn't imagine how a pile of pumpkins could be interesting enough to spend two hours taking pictures of them once, much less twice. But the girls proceeded to do everything over. This time a family with a set of twins in identical green overalls arrived. It added a little life to the scene as they tried to drag a huge pumpkin back to the cash register.

Back at Leslie's house after the second taping, Leslie started trying to convince Erin that the tape was good enough almost before they got it in the machine.

"Look at that color!" she exclaimed. "And that kid with the pumpkin. Isn't he cute? And his face is in focus!"

"But his feet! I cut off his feet," Erin wailed.

"You can't think of everything," Leslie said, shrugging.

They watched the rest of the tape nervously, expecting the worst, but it was a definite improvement over the day before. There were still a few fuzzy spots and too much movement, but there were some good shots, too, especially of the twins, which could be edited into a final version.

"Please, please don't make us go back and

do it again. I can't take any more. Say it's good enough," Leslie said, pleading.

"I guess it'll do," Erin said. "But next time we've got to follow the action better. Those kids kept running out of the picture."

They ran through the footage a few more times, until it was almost six and Erin realized she would be late for dinner if she didn't leave right away.

By the next class meeting, the girls had made their final plans for the second part of their project, a pumpkin-carving party, which would take place in Erin's backyard.

Saturday turned out to be a fine day. Eight of the girls' friends from school showed up, including Jeff whose relationship with Leslie had improved a hundred percent since they had given up trying to be video partners. Each guest brought a pumpkin. Knives, markers, and accessories were provided by the Markssons along with refreshments.

Erin set the camera up next to the picnic table, which had been spread with a thick layer of newspaper, and put the mike in a stand in the center, next to the pile of knives. This time there would be no interviews, just the comments of the kids as they laughed and worked.

The first few minutes were quiet as everybody started in. There was only the steady scrape of the spoons pulling on the pulp.

Erin got a close-up of Leslie's hand sketching a spikey-toothed hag on her pumpkin, then moved on to Jeff's knife as it perfectly traced a rounded eye with a little eyeball at the bottom.

After the gooey piles of pumpkin seeds and soggy newspapers had been cleared from the picnic tables, they lined up all the finished jack-o'-lanterns for a final pan. There was one, wearing a battered straw hat, that looked like a chubby country boy with a round face and wide, innocent eyes. Another was incredibly hideous with long vampire teeth and evil, slanted eyes.

"Leslie, over here!" Erin called as she began unscrewing the camera from the tripod. "We've got enough footage. Help me get this stuff put away before some sort of disaster strikes."

"I bet it makes you nervous when things go this smoothly, doesn't it?" Leslie asked, laughing.

"Don't forget, Davy's still here," Erin said with a grin.

After everyone had gone home the two girls

took the tape to Leslie's house for viewing. They logged the whole thing right then, noting the counter numbers for the beginning and ending of each scene on their logging chart. They admired the good parts, groaned over the bad ones, and discussed ways to do better on the final segment. Their camera work was much smoother now with a few successful zooms. And there was a good variety of types of shots and camera angles. They were definitely improving, but the pace was agonizingly slow.

Erin was constantly seeing things that could be improved in their work. Unfortunately her ideas about what the final product would look like kept well ahead of her ability to actually produce it on tape. So even though each thing they attempted looked better than the last, she was always dissatisfied.

Leslie wasn't quite so unrealistic, reminding Erin of the progress they had made. But Erin was convinced that Leslie was simply more interested in her piano than the video.

For the first time in their lives, Mr. and Mrs. Marksson were urging their daughter to slow down and not work so hard. Her dad even invited her to take an afternoon off from reading technical books on video production to go see a movie with the rest of the family. They had never seen Erin work so hard on anything before, and they were amazed at the sudden change in character.

On Halloween night the girls even skipped a party at the Y so they could get the closing shots of the pumpkins sitting on front porches with hordes of trick-or-treaters streaming past. Leslie took charge of this part, setting up lights to flood her front porch and placing a cute pumpkin on one side and a terrifying one on the other side of the stairs. Then she and Erin spent about fifteen minutes coaching the neighborhood kids on how not to walk into the camera.

After a few run-throughs, the trick-or-treaters cooperated well enough to get some seemingly candid shots. Then they moved on to Jeff's house where his masterpiece was glowing inside the front window. They set up again there and repeated the scene from Leslie's.

"Do you have the energy for one more move?" Erin asked, eyeing the witches and clowns parading down the block.

"I don't think so. I've had it," Leslie replied as she started packing up.

Erin wasn't ready to quit yet. "Come on, just over to my house. It'll take fifteen minutes."

"Okay, but only if we stay and eat your leftover candy. I haven't had my quota of sweets for the night, and I think I need some quick energy."

"It's fine with me, but you may have to fight Davy for it."

"That's all right," Leslie said. "I think I can handle him."

But the hardest part still lay ahead—the hours in the editing booth.

A few days before their project was due, the girls decided to have their families preview the tape. They'd been agonizing over it for so long that they couldn't be objective anymore. The Markssons, along with Jeff and his family, were invited to Leslie's house for dessert and a showing.

After everyone had had seconds on fudge brownies in the kitchen, Leslie called them into the living room, put the tape in the VCR, and pressed the play button.

"Okay, this is it!" Leslie announced.

Everyone dutifully settled down as the camera panned a field of pumpkins to a banjo accompaniment.

"Does anyone hear a buzzing noise?" Davy asked as the video switched to the Markssons' backyard.

"I knew someone would notice it," Erin said to Leslie. "I don't know how that happened," she said. "But we couldn't get rid of it without losing all the sound from this segment."

"That's not important, dear," Mrs. Marksson said reassuringly. "The colors are beautiful."

"We struggled for hours to get it just right," Erin said.

"I can vouch for that," Leslie said. "I worked my fingers to the bone pushing those buttons."

"Shhh!" Davy hissed. "My part's coming up soon!"

Erin couldn't help smiling as her brother appeared on the screen. "You ham," she muttered, wondering if Hollywood directors ever had to put up with little brothers.

"You did a good job, girls," Mr. Marksson said as the credits appeared.

"I'm glad we have a few more days, though," Erin said. "I think we can fix up the part just before the credits a little better."

"Here we go again," Leslie moaned. "Miss Perfectionist. Just don't forget about our deadline." She turned to their parents, explaining, "Eve lowers your grade a whole point if you don't finish on time. She says working with deadlines is the most important thing you can learn in this business."

"Well, I think it's amazing that the two of you have learned so much in such a short time," Leslie's mother said.

Erin was both pleased and disappointed. She was pleased that their families had been so enthusiastic, but she was disappointed that there were so many places where the finished product fell short of her expectations. As she had visualized the finished piece, there were no hums or buzzes, no jumps, no fuzzy focusing or sloppy edits.

But the excitement she had felt sitting with an audience, even the uncritical family group gathered that night, and watching her own tape on TV was unbeatable. She wasn't discouraged, only determined to fix what she could before the deadline and make each tape better than the last.

Chapter Thirteen

On the day the projects were due, Erin nervously handed in the tape and took a seat at the back of the room next to Leslie and Jeff as the other interns filed into the studio.

"I wish we didn't have to show it to the whole class," she said to Leslie. "I hate these discussions when it's my stuff that's up there on the screen."

"Don't worry," Leslie answered confidently. "Everyone will like it. We did a pretty good job, if I do say so myself."

Erin looked doubtful. She knew they had worked hard and done their best, but she still wasn't sure that it was good enough to be submitted for judging at the convention. The best projects from the class were to be entered in a state video contest for student producers, and the whole class was planning to attend the convention at which the winners would be announced.

Eve was in front of the class perched casually on the metal stairs of the light platform, waiting impatiently till the last student closed the door before turning down the lights.

"Okay, folks," she said. "I think we'll start today's session with Erin and Leslie. Could one of you stand up and tell us briefly what you've been up to?"

Leslie nudged Erin. "Go ahead."

"You do it," Erin whispered.

"No, you," Leslie insisted.

Erin hated having to talk about her work, and her voice quavered nervously as she began her short introduction.

Boy, does that sound like a dumb topic, she thought to herself as she sat quickly back down again. *Nobody's going to be interested in pumpkins.* She wondered briefly if it was too late to flee the country. Anything would be better than sitting there, listening to the snickers and smart comments of her classmates. But she stayed glued to her seat. She had to see what their reaction would be.

"Okay. Roll it," Eve called out, signaling to the technician in the control room.

Erin looked intently at the monitor, trying to see the show as if for the first time.

The studio door opened a crack, letting in a sliver of light as Matt entered. He stood in the back for a while, leaning against the wall, not wanting to take the empty seat next to Erin.

The tape started with the stubble of the pumpkin field backed by brilliant amber and red fall foliage, then cut to an overview of the farm stand with people weighing bags of apples and squash, and ended on a huge mountain of pumpkins, which turned the whole screen a fiery orange.

Erin barely saw the screen. All she was aware of was Matt, standing by the door. Finally she couldn't take it any longer. She turned and motioned him to sit down beside her.

Reluctantly he sat down, whispered a quick hello, then turned his full attention to the screen.

The twins were on now, darting from side to side as they played with the pumpkins. Next came a close-up of the cash register ringing up a sale and three nice round pumpkins being placed in a customer's trunk. Then the camera followed the car as it wound down the dirt road past a weathered red barn and grazing cows.

Erin and Matt both stared straight ahead, scarcely acknowledging the other's presence. She tried to think of something to say to ease the tension, but it was Matt who finally broke the silence.

He leaned over and whispered shyly, "This one has some pretty fancy editing. I liked those quick cuts. They were nice and clean."

She could hardly believe her ears. "You think so?"

"Yeah, and the shots of the shoppers weren't bad, either. It's awfully hard to avoid people walking in and out of focus."

The next shot was at the party, a close-up of a knife carving a crooked mouth.

"And the camera work isn't bad, either," Matt went on. "Someone's got a nice, steady hand."

"Uhmmmm," Erin agreed, suddenly realizing that Matt didn't know whose tape it was.

They watched without comment for a few minutes as the scene changed to Halloween night. The background music got louder, and the images began to change in time to the music.

"Nice transitions," Matt said. "I like the way they got those close-ups of the little kids' faces as they were coming down the stairs. The expressions are great."

"That little witch with the frizzy hair is cute, isn't she?" Erin said.

"Hey, that kid in the crazy hat looks like your brother!"

"It is. He was attempting to be a zombie for Halloween this year," Erin said, trying not to smile.

Matt watched silently for a few more minutes until it finally dawned on him what he was watching.

"Erin, this is your tape, isn't it?" he whispered.

She nodded, still concentrating on the screen, scrutinizing every frame.

"Why didn't you say so? It's really good!"

She turned to look at his face as he spoke, still not convinced of his sincerity.

"No, not 'good.' I mean fantastic! Really."

"Let's keep it quiet in the back," Eve said. "We'll discuss it when the tape is over."

As the closing credits flashed on the screen the class began to clap. Erin blushed at the attention, then she and Leslie both stood up, smiled, and took a little bow.

"See, they loved it," Matt said as she sat down again.

"Sure, but what about Eve?" Erin whispered. "You know how she can tear things apart."

But Matt was right. Except for a few minor suggestions, Eve was enthusiastic about the project.

Erin could hardly sit through the other three shows scheduled for that afternoon. There were a million things she wanted to say to Matt.

At last the class was over, and in silent agreement they escaped next door to the privacy of a back booth at the ice cream shop.

The first few minutes were awkward, and Erin stared at the menu for a while before ordering her usual double chocolate sundae. Why did she feel so completely tongue-tied?

"You know, Erin," Matt said after an uncomfortable silence, "I still don't know why you didn't want to finish that festival tape with me. The footage was pretty good, and it seemed like we were getting along fine. Were you mad or something?"

"No, I wasn't mad. Not at you, anyway. You were amazingly understanding, considering the way I was goofing up. Anyone would have been annoyed."

"I guess I did lose my temper once," he admitted. "But I apologized, didn't I? I know how hard it is in the beginning—you think you must be the stupidest person in the world. But I also knew you'd get the hang of it eventually. Just as I did."

"I guess it's hard for me to learn new things," Erin admitted. "I hate to make mistakes. When I first learned to ride a bike, I went to a park way over on the other side of town where none of my friends would see me and practiced by myself every day for a week. At the end of the week I rode all the way home, covered with bandages, but able to ride. I'm sorry I had to quit on you like that. But it was the only way I could do it."

"Well, you're stubborn, that's for sure," he said. "More stubborn than you look." He gazed down into her pale blue eyes and tipped her head up to his.

Erin caught her breath at his touch, leaning forward, till their faces were inches apart. *If only we weren't in public,* she thought, remembering that first wonderful kiss on the river bank.

"You worry too much about being perfect," Matt said gently.

"It's not that. It's—"

"Yes, you do," he insisted. "And it isn't necessary. Don't you know I'm crazy about you just the way you are, mistakes and all?"

Erin felt her eyes filling with tears. "Oh, Matt, I missed you so much."

"Not half as much as I missed you," He leaned forward and kissed her lightly, right there in the middle of the ice-cream parlor! "I'll forgive you for all the grief on one condition."

Erin giggled. "You know, you're not very good at sounding stern."

"One condition."

"What?"

"Promise to be my partner next semester."

"I'll think about it," she told him. And then as he rose over her in mock rage, she said, "All right, all right! Partners." She held out her hand. Matt took it and then sat down, still holding on.

Erin looked at her hand in his. "I think it'd really be fun to work together now," she told him, all teasing gone.

"Good, because I had a hard time going it alone after I found out how much fun it was to work with you." He looked up as the waitress brought their sundaes to the table. "I could've used some company when I did the interview for my project."

"Oh, my gosh! I didn't even ask you about your project! What'd you do?"

"I filmed a guy who paints model soldiers."

"Figures, you'd do something obvious like that," Erin said. "How'd you get that idea?"

"An old friend of my father's has this fantastic collection of miniature lead soldiers. He's a real interesting old guy from Europe with bushy white hair and lots of stories to tell."

"What does he do with them, have pretend battles?" Erin asked, amused at the thought of an elderly man lying on the floor playing with toy soldiers.

"No, he makes new ones and paints them for a hobby. He's interested in military history and he makes models with accurate historical costumes, right down to the color of the buttons. I taped the whole thing in an eight-hour marathon."

"How come it took you eight hours?"

"Well, I wanted to show how he completed one entire figure. Sort of a time-lapse effect. I started as he put on the base colors, then I waited until the paint dried and he started to add detail and shading. In my video you see the figure almost come to life by the end of the tape."

"That sounds great—but complicated."

"Well, it was a tough shoot. I had to use a special close-up lens to get the detail as he painted. Every jiggle of the camera made it look like you were taping on an ocean liner. I could really have used an extra pair of hands, though."

"This pair of extra hands might have brought a little unwelcome excitement," Erin said. "If I'd let you down, you would've been *really* mad."

"You know what, Erin?" Matt said. "I'm not nearly as tough on people as you think I am. You're the one with such high standards—you're much harder on yourself than I would ever be."

Erin winced. "You're probably right. Now that I think about it, I gave poor Leslie a pretty tough time. I was trying so hard to prove that I could do it, I got a little fanatical. We did some of those edits over at least a dozen times."

"I was that way at first, too," Matt admitted. "After a while, though, you get more realistic. You can't get everything perfect in the beginning. When we're partners next semester, we'll have to keep each other in line or we'll never meet our deadlines. There'll always be one last thing to fix."

Erin finished the last of her sundae. "Don't worry. I think I'm cured. This semester has been exhausting. I've never worked so hard at anything in my life. I can't wait for the break so I can have a little fun."

"Why don't we start right now?" Matt stood up and reached for her hand. "Interested in a movie tonight? I've heard that *A Night in Metropolis* has terrific editing."

"Could you do me a favor?" Erin asked as she lightly touched his arm.

"Sure."

"Could we do something that has absolutely nothing to do with video or editing?"

Matt looked at her and laughed. "How about roller-skating?"

"That sounds terrific. Let's go."

Chapter Fourteen

The Saturday after Thanksgiving was the evening of the awards ceremony for the state video contest. When Matt arrived to pick Erin up, she felt a little like Cinderella going to the ball. It was exciting to be invited downtown to the elegant old Copley Square Hotel.

The Oriental carpets and cut-glass chandeliers on the high ceilings ensured that all the interns were on their best behavior. Erin, wearing her most sophisticated dress, a smashing blue silk she had gotten for her rich cousin's wedding, felt she looked more like twenty-one than sixteen. She just hoped she wouldn't do something like use the wrong fork.

After an elegant dinner, the awards ceremony began as the master of ceremonies stepped up to the podium and cleared his throat. He began a dull speech, which Erin barely listened to, and finally reached the part she was waiting for.

"As president of the Massachusetts Association for Video Education, I am happy to recognize the following young artists with an honorable mention. Although there is no monetary prize attached to this award, it does indicate significant overall achievement in the field of video production. Would the following students please rise. . . ."

The speaker read six names, each followed by polite applause. Then came number seven, Leslie D'Amico, and number eight, Erin Marksson. The New England Cable interns clapped and cheered as their classmates rose to acknowledge the award. The two girls exchanged proud smiles and hugs.

The ceremony continued as third and second prizes were announced for the various categories and the remaining nominees were left to wonder who would get the coveted first prize. Only Erin felt sure she knew who it would be.

Finally she heard the words, "I'd like to

present Matthew Richard Blakeslee, from New England Cable, with this five-hundred-dollar scholarship award for his winning entry in the Documentary Division, *The Steadfast Soldier.* Congratulations, Matt. Keep up the good work."

When the applause finally died down, Erin was the last one to stop clapping. Her eyes followed Matt's charcoal-gray suit as he slowly threaded his way through the crowded tables to the podium to accept the award.

"Thank you very much," Matt said from the platform. He was looking, it seemed to Erin, directly at her as he spoke. "I'd like to thank Eve Stratford and her staff and every-one at NEC who made it as much fun to make this tape as I hope it will be to watch it."

"Now we'll see Matt's entry," the announcer said.

As the tape was screened on the four moni-tors ringing the hotel dining room, Erin couldn't take her eyes off Matt. She had never seen him look so handsome.

There was more applause as the tape ended and Matt stepped down, proudly holding up his certificate and check as he made his way back to his seat among the Ashboro interns.

"Congratulations, you got *first!*" Jeff said, slapping him on the back.

"I didn't think it was that great," Matt protested, grinning.

"It was terrific and you know it," said Leslie, who was sitting on the other side of Erin. "It was ten times better than anything in our class."

"I don't know about that," Matt said. "I think yours should have at least tied."

"I'm perfectly satisfied with honorable mention," Erin said. "This time, that is. But watch out next year!"

"The competition *is* getting pretty stiff around here," Eve added, smiling. "You've all come a long way. Now all you have to do is keep up the good work."

After the ceremony Erin and Matt left the hotel and walked into Copley Square. They stood on the steps in front of the stately old public library building, gazing at the sparkling white lights that decorated the leafless trees lining the square. The holiday decorations had already begun to appear: green-boughed wreaths hung from the lanternstyle lamps along the paths, and the fancy boutiques on Newberry Street housed the gold-and-silver elegance of Christmas displays.

"Let's look at the windows," Matt suggested, "if you're not too cold."

"Sure," Erin answered as she buttoned up her gray wool coat tightly around her neck and stuck her gloved hands deep into the side pockets.

As they strolled along in the brisk night air, Matt's arm, which had been around Erin's shoulder, dropped down to her waist, and his hand found its way into her pocket. He curled his hand around hers for warmth.

"Let me in, too. I forgot my gloves," he said, bending down till his lips touched her cold nose.

Before she could answer, he stooped lower and covered her mouth with his. They clung together for a moment, Matt's strong arms encircling hers. Then he pulled off her knitted hat and ran his fingers through the silky golden strands of hair that whipped back and forth on her neck in the brisk night breeze.

Erin felt the tips of her ears turning pink with cold. But it didn't matter. The rest of her was melting in the warm, sweet glow of Matt's love.

ANNOUNCING THE SPECTACULAR

ALL THAT GLITTERS

SWEEPSTAKES

It's part of the hot new series **ALL THAT GLITTERS**. In each book you'll meet the cast of the sensational soap opera **ALL THAT GLITTERS** and share the joys and heartaches as they balance their acting careers with the ups and downs of teenage life.

THREE CHANCES TO WIN!

Not just Book #1, but **Books #2 & 3 as well** offer you a chance at fabulous prizes! In the back of each book will be a question about that story—and if you are among the first five hundred to submit a correct entry you will win a fantastic ALL THAT GLITTERS "EARLY BIRD PRIZE". 1500 PRIZES—500 EARLY BIRD PRIZES AWARDED FOR EACH BOOK!

BUT THE BEST IS YET TO COME!

Every correct entry from the three books will be entered in our Grand Prize Sweepstakes—and the winner will win A TRIP FOR TWO TO NEW YORK CITY (3 DAYS/2 NIGHTS) INCLUDING HOTEL . . . TRANSPORTATION AND DINNERS.

No purchase necessary. Sweepstakes ends January 31st, 1988. Entry blanks and official rules will be found in the back of MAGIC TIME #1, TAKE TWO #2, and FLASHBACK #3 or see special displays wherever books are sold for complete details, including alternative means of entry.

Don't miss your chance! Book #1, Magic Time, will be on sale in September—and watch closely for Book #2 (on sale October) and Book #3 (on sale November).

ALL THAT GLITTERS

It's Hot!

Get Ready for a Thrilling Time in Sweet Valley®!

☐ **26905 DOUBLE JEOPARDY #1**   **$2.95**

When the twins get part-time jobs on the Sweet Valley newspaper, they're in for some chilling turn of events. The "scoops" Jessica invents to impress a college reporter turn into the real thing when she witnesses an actual crime—but now no one will believe her! The criminal has seen her car, and now he's going after Elizabeth ... the twins have faced danger and adventure before ... but never like this!

Prices and availability subject to change without notice.

Buy them at your local bookstore or use this handy coupon for ordering:

SWEET DREAMS are fresh, fun and exciting—alive with the flavor of the contemporary teen scene—the joy and doubt of *first love*. If you've missed any SWEET DREAMS titles, then you're missing out on *your* kind of stories, written about people like *you*!

☐	25814	PRIVATE EYES #113 Julia Winfield	$2.50
☐	25815	JUST THE WAY YOU ARE #114 Janice Boies	$2.50
☐	26158	PROMISE ME LOVE #115 Jane Redish	$2.50
☐	26195	HEARTBREAK HILL #116 Carol MacBain	$2.50
☐	26196	THE OTHER ME #117 Terri Fields	$2.50
☐	26293	HEART TO HEART #118 Stefanie Curtis	$2.50
☐	26339	STAR-CROSSED LOVE #119 Sharon Cadwallader	$2.50
☐	26340	MR. WONDERFUL #120 Fran Michaels	$2.50
☐	26418	ONLY MAKE-BELIEVE #121 Julia Winfield	$2.50
☐	26419	STARS IN HER EYES #122 Dee Daley	$2.50
☐	26481	LOVE IN THE WINGS #123 Virginia Smiley	$2.50
☐	26482	MORE THAN FRIENDS #124 Janice Boies	$2.50
☐	26528	PARADE OF HEARTS #125 Cloverdale Press	$2.50
☐	26566	HERE'S MY HEART #126 Stefanie Curtis	$2.50
☐	26567	MY BEST ENEMY #127 Janet Quin-Harkin	$2.50
☐	26671	ONE BOY AT A TIME #128 Diana Gregory	$2.50
☐	26672	A VOTE FOR LOVE #129 Terri Fields	$2.50
☐	26701	DANCE WITH ME #130 Jahnna Beecham	$2.50
☐	26865	HAND-ME-DOWN HEART #131 Mary Schultz	$2.50
☐	26790	WINNER TAKES ALL #132 Laurie Lykken	$2.50
☐	26864	PLAYING THE FIELD #133 Eileen Hehl	$2.50
☐	26789	PAST PERFECT #134 Fran Michaels	$2.50

Prices and availability subject to change without notice.